Angels and Shadows Sexy Surprises

Sexy Surprises, Volume 28

Giselle Renarde

Published by Giselle Renarde, 2023.

Table of Contents

Angels and Shadows
Sexy Surprises

6 Erotic Stories
Giselle Renarde

Wonderful Wing Boys

Deb walked right by the entrance, though she'd been inside this building many times before. Her whole world changed when the office gave her this Smartphone thingy. She never fell out of touch anymore, always had her eyes glued to its little screen, always had her fingers perched over its keys.

She'd thought she was too old for new tricks, too old to keep up with technology, but not so. Once her assistant had explained it to her, she realized what a godsend this device really was.

Yanking open the heavy wooden door, Deb avoided the layers of peeling paint and trotted to the dark staircase. She held the railing with one hand, still entrenched in emails. Deb knew which stair was broken, and counted in her mind so she could step over it when she got there.

Another message came in before she'd even finished reading the last one—wasn't that always the way?

"Good evening, Deb."

She barely looked up from the glowing screen to nod in the doorman's direction. Short guy, but built like an ox. His strong arms were perpetually crossed in front of his barrel chest.

Deb never could remember his name.

"The Big Guy's not down that way," he said.

Deb overshot the club's entrance and traced familiar footsteps down the dark hallway leading to the office. She didn't stop at first, because she wasn't really listening. When the words finally sunk in, she turned around.

"He's in the club?" she asked.

That was strange. She thought The Big Guy didn't buy into his own hype.

When Deb looked up from her phone, she realized the doorman was shaking his head.

"The Big Guy has left the building," he informed her.

This had to be some kind of joke, and yet the Asian doorman's handsome, chubby face remained expressionless.

"What do you mean he left?" Deb asked, scrolling through her messages. She clicked on the appointment reminder The Big Guy's assistant had sent early in the afternoon. "It says right here we're scheduled to go over the zoning variance applications."

Not the sort of thing Deb would generally have done in person... in this part of town... at ten o'clock at night... but for The Big Guy, she made all kinds of exceptions.

The doorman shrugged those hulking bare shoulders, and his huge white wings stretched out behind him. It was a strangely cat-like move, when the boys flicked their wings like that. In fact, Deb felt a little strange that these handsome supernatural creatures didn't inspire more awe.

Maybe something was missing inside of her.

It wasn't common for humans to come in close contact with actual angels. This club, created by The Big Guy to serve a clientele of women in Deb's age bracket, was incredibly exclusive. It was an invite-only sort of deal, and the only reason Deb knew about it was her work with zoning ordinances.

Yes, even The Big Guy had to abide by city by-laws when operating on their turf.

The first time she'd come here, she was all business. There was no real reason to leave The Big Guy's office, but he'd taken her on a tour of the club nonetheless, so she would know exactly what she was dealing with.

The club was called Only Angels, and for a good reason: all the guys who worked the place were honest-to-goodness angelic beings.

Her ulcer had just about blinded her with pain that day. Obviously, that had cut the tour short. It was only when she got home later, pulled on her flannel pyjamas and grabbed a tub of Triple Caramel Chunk from the freezer, that she realized the enormous implications of everything she'd seen.

Those boys were angels, wings and everything!

It beggared belief, and yet Deb trusted things that were tangible, palpable, firm—and, man, those angel boys were about as firm as they come!

Ever since that first meeting, The Big Guy had nudged Deb to check out the club every time she swung by his office. She always had some excuse not to. Hell, they had a lot of work to do with this variance application, and The Big Guy wasn't her only client. There was an entire city's worth of zoning to take care of, and nobody else in her department knew what the hell they were doing. She couldn't trust the work to anyone but herself.

Now, as she stood in this dark and dreary hallway in the basement of a deceptively run-down building, it dawned on her what must be going on.

She watched as the doorman's wings settled into resting position behind his back.

"The Big Guy couldn't have just taken off," she told him. "We've had this appointment on the books for weeks."

Deb glared at the doorman, trying to read his blank expression.

"What did he tell you when he left?"

The doorman smiled, an almost canine grin, like he just couldn't help himself. "The Big Guy instructed me to send you into the club. Andreas and Zander would like to consult with you."

A set-up if ever she saw one!

Still, she couldn't keep the smirk from her lips. "Do Andreas and Zander wish to bone up on their knowledge of zoning by-laws?"

With a chuckle that made his shoulders heave, the doorman said, "I'm sure they'd gladly bone *something*."

A long-forgotten pulse grabbed Deb between the legs. For a moment, she felt so weak she just about keeled over. She looked at her phone. Ten at night and messages were still popping up at the top of her inbox, knocking the older ones out of sight.

"I've got so much left to do today..."

She looked to the doorman, hoping he'd offer her a reason to stay.

"Zander and Andreas are waiting in booth six," he said, his voice a low rumble she could feel in her belly. "They're yours for the night, courtesy of The Big Guy."

He swung the door open and stepped aside.

She beamed at the angel as she walked by. No sense pretending she wouldn't enjoy an evening of reckless debauchery.

"Tell The Big Guy thanks, will you?"

"What," he teased, "you can't just send The Big Guy a thank you message on that little machine of yours?"

Laughing along, Deb said, "I could, but some things are nicer in person."

When he'd closed the first door behind her, Deb leaned against it and shut her eyes. She knew this feeling—she was nervous.

Nervous!

At her age it seemed silly, but the truth was she hadn't been with a man since her husband left, and that was years ago. Even then, her work had always come first. Her kids, even as adults, wouldn't let her live down the number of sports games and school concerts she'd missed when they were young. They seemed to think those choices had been easy. They seemed to think that if she had to do it all over again, she'd make the same choices.

She wouldn't. She knew that now.

Deb opened her eyes and gazed into the fountain at the centre of the small room. The water's musical chime eased that tumbling feeling in her stomach, and its fresh springtime scent made her thirsty for something more than a drink. She walked the little pathway around the water feature and took a deep breath before opening the next door.

There were loads of women at the bar, even on a Wednesday. They were so glamorous, each on the arm of a young angel... or two or three. *Cougar sluts*, Deb had thought the first time she came here. That was before The Big Guy told her these women wearing gold mini-skirts and sequin tops that barely kept their boobs covered, didn't dress this way to go to work in the morning. Many of them were respectable businesswomen, or lonely society ladies, or down-on-their-luck single mothers who worked their fingers to the bone while their grown children sat at home playing video games.

Every woman here had at least one thing in common: a need.

For a long time, Deb had resisted hers, but The Big Guy obviously wasn't buying the act.

Avoiding the bar, Deb squeezed past working hunks and their huge white wings to get to the booths. Most of the white curtains were closed, which meant an angel was inside entertaining a client. When she arrived at booth six, she found the ceiling-to-floor curtain shut. Her angels must have closed it so the boss wouldn't think they were slacking off.

That's what she was thinking to herself as she pulled the curtain wide open.

Deb gasped at what she saw.

She told herself to pull the curtain closed again, but she couldn't manage it. Two angels—one dark-skinned with full pouting lips and the other golden with long black hair—were sitting together on the U-shaped bench. Kissing. Not only were they kissing, but touching, their hands travelling the terrain of each other's chests and arms. Deb was pretty sure they were stroking lower, too, but she couldn't fully see because of the round table blocking her view.

The darker of the angels was the first to notice her. His big brown eyes grew wide, and he quickly pushed the other guy away, hissing, "Get off me! She's here!"

The second angel met Deb's bewildered gaze with a sheepish expression of his own. "Hello," he said. A distinct blush grew across his cheeks. "I must apologize for Zander's and my naughty antics. We didn't know how long you would be and we found ourselves getting rather... frisky..."

Both angels spoke with delicious accents. Andreas's sounded South American to her ear, but she wasn't exactly sure about Zander. African-French was her best guess. The chiming water outside the bar had made her feel peaceful, but the men's voices produced an altogether different effect. She felt riled up, vicious and eager, like she wanted to pounce.

Andreas stood and extended his hand to Deb. As he rose, his hard cock sprung out from his open fly. Deb could hardly believe it when she heard herself giggle like a schoolgirl.

"Pleased to meet you," she said, foregoing his hand and wrapping her fingers around his firm, uncut cock instead. It throbbed against her palm as she said, "I'm Deb."

The boy gasped, then chuckled like a nervous teenager.

"The Big Guy had many wonderful things to say about you," Andreas assured her while he shyly extracted his erection from her grip. He sunk down onto the bench.

"Spoiled sport," she teased, closing the white curtain and ducking in beside Zander. She snuck a peek at his fly, but he'd already zipped it up.

They both wore tight white jeans and were both bare-chested, which was part of the uniform here at Only Angels. Most human shirts didn't fit too well over a massive set of wings.

"Sorry to interrupt," Deb said. "You two were obviously in the middle of something."

"The thought of your arrival made us both so horny we just couldn't resist—"

"Bullshit," Deb interrupted, laughing. "You guys make each other horny. That's obvious enough."

Her Smartphone sang a little tune to tell her she had a new message, but she turned the damn thing off and slipped it into her jacket pocket.

No interruptions tonight.

Ignoring her comment, Zander said, "Andreas and I are yours for the evening, to use as you wish. Would you like a drink to start things off? Or something to eat, perhaps?"

Deb laughed. "Food has been my only pleasure for years. Can't you tell?"

The boys chuckled politely. Of course they weren't going to answer that question.

"It's been ages since I've indulged anything but my taste buds," Deb went on. "My other senses are very jealous."

"What shall we do about that?" Zander asked. He put an arm around her shoulder and she couldn't believe the heat coming off the guy.

Andreas grinned like a schoolboy and finished the thought. "Or should we just show you what we have to give?"

They probably worked tag team like this often, if they were able to finish each other's sentences.

Or maybe they were in love...

Zander must have perceived a shift in Deb's bearing, because he let his arm slide from her shoulder. Setting both hands on the table, he leaned forward and tilted his head. "A lot of women we meet want to talk for a while. That's fine, too."

Deb smiled at his sweetness. "Oh, you really do know women, don't you, boys?"

The pair exchanged apprehensive glances.

"We try," Andreas replied.

"But you understand one another even better," Deb went on. She wasn't usually so perceptive, but there was such a strong connection between the two she couldn't bring herself to ignore it.

The boys looked at each other once again, eyes wide, as though they were afraid of what she might do with this information.

"Is it obvious?" they asked in unison.

The question made Deb laugh. They were delicious, these two. "Well, when I find the two of you kissing and groping in a closed booth, it tells me something, all right!"

Andreas's cheeks were beet red. Deb had never seen any man look so embarrassed... or any angel.

"We apologize," Zander cut in. "We were supposed to entertain you, and instead ..." He trailed off like he wasn't exactly sure what was happening.

"Oh, I am entertained." Deb tapped Zander's thigh with her hand. "Well, I shouldn't say that. Makes it sound like you're circus bears or something."

"We're hardly bears," Andreas said with a sly smile.

Zander laughed. "Yes, we are far too hairless."

It finally clicked that they were making reference to gay terminology—bears as hairy, hefty gay men. What would Andreas and Zander be considered? The only other word Deb knew was "twinks," but these boys were too firm and fit to fall into that category.

"You won't tell The Big Guy, will you?" Andreas pleaded, his expression suddenly stricken.

His fear inspired a surge of warmth around Deb's heart, and she reached for both their hands. "You think The Big Guy doesn't already know?"

They looked at one another, so sheepish, so adorable.

"I guess there's no hiding from The Big Guy," Zander conceded.

"You got that right." Deb gently placed Zander's hand in Andreas's palm, and smiled at the happy image of two men in love.

"It's not that we don't enjoy women," Zander said. The statement seemed to come out of nowhere, but Deb understood that these boys took their occupation seriously. "We love working here at Only Angels. The only thing we don't like is hiding that we enjoy each other, too."

"Oh, you darling boys!" Deb couldn't help leaning across the table and throwing her arms around them both. They'd only just met, but she felt like she'd known them forever. "You don't have to hide with me. I see how much you care for each other, and I love your love!" Eagerness burned through her body. "I want to *see* your love. *Show* it to me."

The very idea made her throb between the thighs, but the angels looked surprised. Or scared, maybe?

Zander met her gaze first. "You don't mean…?"

"Yes," she said, kissing his forehead and then Andreas's. "Is that strange? Other women don't make these requests?"

"It's never really been on the menu," Andreas admitted. "But we could add it, for you."

His words made her feel like the most special woman in the club. Nobody else was going to witness what she would tonight.

When the angels stood, their firm bodies sent a tingle through Deb's core.

"What's your favourite thing to do together?" she asked. "That's what I want to see."

She leaned her elbow on the table, resting her chin against her palm. One of Zander's wings was so close to her face it tickled her cheek. He reached for Andreas' cock, which had softened while they spoke and now hung loose against his white denim, down past the V of his open fly. The moment Zander touched that flaccid shaft, it perked noticeably.

The angels each had one foot on the ground and the other knee resting on the booth's padded bench. Everything in here was white, and the boys' bodies popped against that muted backdrop. Deb really couldn't believe how handsome they were, with those big shoulders, rippled abdomens, muscular arms.

The Big Guy sure knew how to pick 'em. This club truly was heaven on earth!

Andreas gripped the back of the bench with one hand while Zander coaxed his sleeping cock awake. Deb couldn't decide which was more alluring, the sight of Zander manhandling Andreas, or the view of Zander's pleasure hidden beyond those tight jeans. To her eyes, it was a massive throb of white denim, tucked to the left and extending like a thick branch down his thigh.

She felt compelled to touch it, but she waited, expecting Andreas to make the first move. Andreas, however, seemed lost in a world of his own, eyes closed, mouth agape in ecstasy. His head tilted to one side, and his long hair hung loose over his shoulder.

That image of masculine enjoyment made her dizzy. She was sure she could taste the testosterone on the air, like a lingering aroma of meat and salt and sweat. She swallowed again and again, devouring it.

Deb was shocked by her body's impulse. Her fingers didn't ask permission to press against the bulge in Zander's jeans, but she forgave them when he awarded her with a moan.

Gazing softly from Andreas's cock to Deb's fingers, Zander grinned and said, "Rub harder."

The feel of that hardness under her palm, even separated by a layer of denim, unleashed a throbbing ache between Deb's thighs. As she stroked him, she felt an equal throb in his body.

Her impulse was to tear into his pants, but zippers could be treacherous. Gingerly, she unbuttoned him, unzipped him, and reached into his pants. They were so tight there was scarcely room for his dick and her hand to co-exist.

Wrangling his hardness, she pulled it from his fly, cupping his big balls in one hand. There was something about male parts, about the feel of that unique heat against her palm, that sent her senses reeling. It had been so long, but the knowledge came screaming back as her fingers wrapped around Zander's length.

"Let me show you something," Zander offered. When she tried to extract her ball-cupping hand from his pants, he said, "No, leave it."

Following his simple instruction, Deb sat in quiet awe and watched as Zander pulled Andreas's foreskin back and made their gleaming cockheads kiss.

Andreas's eyes shot open and he looked down, chuckling, "Oh yeah!" like he was in disbelief.

She watched as Andreas took over rubbing his own cock, and found herself gasping when he folded the flesh of his foreskin all the way over Zander's cockhead. She'd never seen anything like it. Must have felt damn good, judging by the way both angels moaned.

Andreas wrapped his fist around their two cockheads, which were now both enveloped by foreskin. He began a slight stroking motion, twisting his wrist as he rubbed.

Deb couldn't help wondering what that would feel like. She'd give just about anything to experience the kind of sensation men enjoyed during sex. What must it be like to have a massive erection jutting out in front of your body, wrapping your whole hand around its girth, and stroking?

The idea made her weak with arousal.

Zander took the base of his cock in one hand while he pushed down his jeans with the other. Deb helped him out, pulling with one hand while squeezing his balls with the other. Those jeans were so tight they clung to his thighs. The seams left indentations in Zander's beautiful black skin.

Deb didn't realize she'd leaned forward to lick his tight buns until her tongue was lapping that beautiful cheek.

Letting out a chuckling sort of moan, Zander asked, "What would you like, Deb?"

Oh, that buttery accent!

"Anything!" she cried.

Pressing her face into the small of his back, she planted kisses against his salty-sweet skin. Feathers tickled her cheeks and her neck as his wings fluttered gently, cradling her. When was the last time she'd felt so cared for?

Zander hiked her up on the table without so much as breaking the cock connection he shared with Andreas.

Deb hoped to hell this furniture was stable.

"Do you enjoy being penetrated?" Zander asked.

That sequence of words was like an orgasm all over her body. She hardly knew how to answer.

"It was never my favourite," she said. "But I'm in the mood today. Must be the two of you getting me all worked up."

"How do you usually get worked up?" Andreas asked. He was squeezing both their cockheads now, moving his hand in quick, pulsing motions, releasing Zander from the hold of his foreskin, then wrapping that cockhead back up in it. Zander's pinky-brown tip disappeared and reappeared so rapidly it all became a blur.

Instead of answering the question Andreas had asked, Deb growled, "I want those cocks inside of me!"

Peeling off her clothes with incredible ease, she tossed them aside and lay back on her elbows, legs parted widely. There must be something in the air here at Only Angels, because anywhere else she'd have felt extremely self-conscious. In fact, anywhere else she'd never have taken off her clothes in the first place, not in front of two hot young men, and certainly not with the lights on!

Now she spread herself out like a delicacy. "If you can tear yourselves away from each other for a moment, how would you like to try me on for size?"

When they turned to face her, their cocks sprang apart with an almost comical elasticity. They both zeroed in on her exposed pussy.

She reached down to touch it while they watched, their gazes easing her path, making her feel like a goddess. When she let her fingers strum her clit, she was amazed by the power of that sensation. She used to try touching herself, after the ex took off, but nothing ever happened. It never felt good, and she only wound up getting annoyed that she couldn't function sexually, not even on her own. Now, with all the build-up, her pussy was wet and engorged, just begging for someone to show it some love.

Grabbing her thighs with both hands, Zander pulled her into the saddle of his hips. Andreas took the opportunity to sit on the booth bench and shift to her side.

She gasped when he leaned forward to lick her nipple.

God, she'd forgotten how good that felt!

He reached for her far breast, thumbing it as he sucked the closer one. There were so many things she usually hated about her body, but in that moment all she could see was the pleasure of two boys taking her.

As Zander pressed his cockhead firm against her clit, Deb sucked cool air in through her teeth. He rubbed it in tight circles. She couldn't believe how incredible that felt, the smooth flesh of his tip stroking her sensitive bud. She felt hot all over.

And then something flashed across her mind, and she heard herself asking about condoms and the like. Not that she was terribly worried about birth control at her age, but with all you hear about diseases and such she wanted to play it safe.

"We're angels," Zander reminded her. "Not humans. Nothing can pass between us, aside from pleasure."

In response, Andreas went at her nipple even harder, then stood to get the other one in his mouth. When he'd risen, his beautiful cock popped up from under the table and Deb found herself extending her tongue to catch.

Just as Zander eased that steel heat into her pussy, Andreas shifted just enough that she could reach him with her tongue. Grabbing his cock, she pulled the foreskin back and lapped his angelic precum.

The taste was beyond belief, like sugar cookies. She sucked that big boy while Zander issued shallow thrusts inside of her. The teasing made her crazy, and she bucked her hips in his direction, planting her feet against the table edge for support.

With a less-than-angelic growl, Zander pulled Deb into the saddle of his hips. She groaned around Andreas's cock, glad to have something muffling the sounds of her pleasure.

As Zander's thick pulse filled her, she felt time and place slipping away. God, it had been so long. She'd forgotten that it was possible to feel transported to another plane of existence in the arms of a good man... or, in this case, the arms of two gorgeous angels.

Letting Andreas's cock slip out of her mouth, she ran her lips back and forth against his wet shaft. It throbbed in her hand, whacking her face like it had a mind of its own while Andreas observed, laughing. She met his gaze and winked before opening her mouth around that hard thing, cradling it precariously between two sets of teeth.

"Ohhh," Andreas growled. "You wouldn't."

Deb wiggled her eyebrows, teasing.

Zander thrust inside her pussy, making her feel bold and strong. He watched keenly, egging her on: "Yeah, that's right! Bite my boy! Just a little one to keep him humble."

Andreas laughed, shaking his head with an expression of disbelief painted across his face. "You'd never really do it."

That was all the persuasion she needed.

Firmly but gently, Deb closed her mouth around Andreas's shaft, letting just the tips of her teeth sink into his hot flesh.

She didn't take her eyes off him, and neither did Zander as he settled deep inside her unknown realms. When he rolled his hips, his cockhead carved a circular path so far within her body she wasn't quite sure where he was.

A glowing sort of pleasure buzzed at the base of her pelvis, expanding with every rotation of Zander's thick cock. He was inside her, truly inside, in every sense and with every implication that carried. They were connected now and forever. Even when she returned to life and work and daily aggravations, there would always be an angel inside.

The experience was so profound it shifted something in her mind or her heart—hard to tell which—and suddenly she didn't want to bite Andreas anymore. She didn't want to risk hurting him, or anyone, ever.

No, what she really wanted was to give him was pleasure beyond his wildest dreams. Did angels have dreams? Strange, all the things she didn't know about these beautiful boys. Still, that didn't stop her from feeling a glowing affection for them—for the whole world, in fact.

Who'd have thought sex could have such a profound impact?

Releasing her teeth's tender hold, Deb slipped Andreas's cock into the hungry warmth of her mouth, still holding tight to the root of him. He moved gently against her tongue while Zander grasped her ankles, placing them over his shoulders so she could cross them behind his head. She felt incredibly tight like this, with her thighs all pressed together and her bum raised off the table. Hard to believe Zander could support her so effortlessly, but that just went to show how strong he truly was.

When Zander moved inside of her, thrusting hard, his thighs slapped her ass. That wet smacking sound of flesh on flesh made her feel all kinds of naughty, and she sucked harder on the cock she'd all but forgotten. Andreas showed his appreciation by tweaking her nipple, sending shockwaves down to her clit, urging her to buck against Zander's hips, despite her lack of mobility in this upside-down position.

Deb hadn't realized how truly aroused her body had become until Andreas's firm fingers found their way to her clit. That wonderful wing boy parted her lips a touch so she could see Zander's dark cock disappearing.

Tightening her grip around Andreas's shaft, she sucked him with yet more vigour, urging him to come. While feathers shook like autumn leaves, she wondered what an angel's cum would taste like.

Building suction on Andreas's cockhead, she rubbed his shaft at lightning speed. She felt his smooth, wet foreskin gathering at her lips with every stroke.

Zander was digging his fingers into the flesh of her thighs when Andreas's stomach muscles began to ripple and shiver. He tossed his head around, eyes closed, mouth gaping, shining black hair slipping like oil against those gorgeous white wings.

The sight of that sexy man's arousal and the inevitability of his orgasm encouraged Deb to suck even harder. In truth, she wanted to come when he did. Maybe Zander could see that in her face, because he pressed the pad of his thumb against her clit and rubbed it in concentrated circles.

Deb tightened her grip on both their cocks, watching Zander throw his head back and moan. She couldn't believe it—both of her angels were going to come, and if Zander kept at her clit just like that, rubbing round and round at just the right speed and pressure, she was going to come with them!

The moment itself was too explosive to forget, and yet too intense to relive with any semblance of accuracy. Though the pleasure centered in her pussy, she felt a buzz throughout her body. It was so intense she could actually *hear* it.

She was bucking fully off the table now, impaling herself on Zander's cock like gravity had ceased to exist, crying out all the while, "God, yes! Fuck me, fuck me, fuck me, boys! God, I want it now!"

And then the real noise started: a competition of whinnies and grunts from Zander while Andreas erupted in her mouth. The first blast was a hot shock even though she sensed it coming. His cream blasted down her throat, and it wasn't until the secondary jets landed against her tongue that she discovered how wonderful an angel's cum tasted: sweet, maybe a little buttery, with hints of cinnamon.

If only human men tasted so good!

When Andreas pulled his cock away from her eager mouth, she didn't want to let go. And then, just as Zander launched himself so deep inside her she was convinced he'd never find his way out, Andreas leaned in, brushing Zander's thumb away. His dark hair spilled across her belly. Feathers from his huge wing tickled her cheek as his mouth landed like liquid fire against her clit.

Oh, this was it...

Writhing against Andreas's tongue, Deb ran her hands through that gorgeous head of hair. She bunched its silky strands in her fists, tugging hard enough to hurt a man, but not an angel. Andreas just kept licking her, the meat of his hot tongue moving side to side against her clit while Zander fucked her, head back, eyes squeezed shut.

Could Andreas taste Zander's cock down there? His tongue would be so close, so blissfully close to that surging black shaft. The very idea made Deb quiver. Her pussy locked on Zander's cock, milking it, and when she cried out with pleasure he did too—one huge, shared expulsion of naughty words and brutal grunts.

They were animals, all three of them.

In no time, the divine pleasure slipped down that precipice to over-stimulation. Deb writhed on the table, pressing Andreas's tongue and Zander's spent cock away from her worn-out pussy. She couldn't stop panting, and neither could they.

When the angels huddled together on the bench, Deb let her feet rest on their thighs and watched them from the table. She hadn't yet recovered enough energy to sit up, and she couldn't remember the last time she'd felt so liberated lying naked in front of anyone.

Tucking her arm behind her head, Deb watched the boys kiss. Their soft pink lips smiled as they met, sharing a special knowledge. They looked so good together, those two. If her mind wasn't so muddled with the aftershocks of orgasm, she might have wondered why The Big Guy had chosen to pair them with her tonight. No doubt they were supposed to learn some lesson or other. The Big Guy wasn't all about rampant power and control—he really did care about people.

"That was amazing," Deb said, sharing voyeuristically in the angels' embrace. "You guys are incredible. Passion like that..." She shook her head against her arm. "It's something you can't fake."

The angels laughed in unison, and Andreas said, "Very true."

When she slipped her arm out from behind her head and she reached for them, each took a hand, gazing into her eyes like she was really something special.

She couldn't help smiling.

"I'm sure The Big Guy knows," she assured them. "That's probably why he asked you to... well, 'double-team' me or whatever you'd call it."

Andreas and Zander exchanged sheepish grins while they kissed her fingers. Their lips were warm as kitten's paws, and the tenderness of the moment filled her heart.

"You really think so?" Zander asked. "I do love working here at Only Angels, but I also love..." He took a sharp breath in, and looked quickly to Andreas.

With an impish grin, Andreas said, "I love you, too."

Deb rubbed her bare feet against their muscular thighs as they kissed, feeling like she'd helped them, somehow.

Eventually she'd have to roll off this table and into her street clothes. She'd go out into that dark hallway and ascend the broken staircase, push open the door covered in peeling paint, and walk down the alley that always smelled like stagnant rainwater and pee. That was the real world.

Thankfully, she'd have these angels with her all the while. Their love was inside of her now. No matter where she was in the world, they'd always have each other.

© 2011 Giselle Renarde

Skyggen, the Shadow Woman

As dusk came on like a gentle dew, Mirjam sat on the upper terrace of her rustic vacation villa. Sipping local berry wine, she gazed down at the villagers sauntering up the steep incline outside her door. The distance she'd put between herself and urban anxieties made Mirjam feel as though she'd stepped into the past. She could certainly get used to this life.

A yellow bird tore across Mirjam's line of vision, drawing her gaze to the terrace across the street. Her heart jumped in her chest as she jumped out of her wicker chair, splashing wine down the front of her sundress. After a stunned moment of concentrating on the sight that had brought her to her feet, she laughed. It wasn't at all what she thought. She could have sworn she'd caught a glimpse of a dark ghostly woman on the terrace across the street.

Feeling rather sheepish, she realized the form was in fact her own shadow cast outward by the firelight illuminating her villa.

In fact, when she looked very hard, she could see the neighbouring villa was entirely uninhabited. No furnishings, no people, no life. With an intoxicated chuckle, she shook the wine from her dress and stepped inside to change.

When Mirjam took coffee the next morning, she was stunned to find the villa across the way bustling with activity.

Movers brought in the kind of gaudy, over-priced furnishings so often purchased by rich people with no taste. Friends brought baskets of fruits and confectionaries. All activity seemed centred around one woman, who coasted from room to room like a shadow.

AFTER MIRJAM'S VACATION ended, she returned to her life in the city. At first, she thought it was the readjustment to urbanity that had her feeling out of sorts. But, as time passed and her system seemed never to conform to the old way of doing things, she wondered precisely what had happened in that holiday villa to change her personality so drastically.

Suddenly, she couldn't stand the career that had keenly held her interest for so many years. She gave up gambling for charity work and alcohol for spiritual involvement. She took up yoga and meditation, took on a vegetarian diet, and still she felt in some sense incomplete.

Though her body was healthier than ever, her conscience grew heavier by the day. She became pale and thin. The evil career was killing her, she decided, and so she quit.

She'd seen every doctor, who'd attributed her condition to ennui and a whole host of other intangible diseases. They prescribed every medication imaginable, but Mirjam no longer believed in the usefulness of pills. She knew her health had deteriorated for some mysterious internal reason, and could not be restored until she knew the cause.

In the meantime, her cheeks grew gaunt and her muscles weakened. As her physical condition deteriorated, Mirjam's mind brought her back to the daytime heat of her provincial villa and the firelight at dusk. She smiled as she recollected spilling wine across her dress that day she was spooked by her own shadow. Her stomach quaked.

As Mirjam lay her head to rest one evening, a commotion in the hallway outside her apartment jolted her awake. She couldn't make out the words spoken, but one of the voices seemed particularly familiar. Perhaps she'd steal a peek through the peephole, to find out what the ruckus was all about.

The very moment Mirjam crept out of bed, her front door burst open. Her heart stopped. She tried to scream, but her voice lodged itself so deep in her throat she nearly choked.

The figure in the doorway didn't look much like a cat burglar, but Mirjam knew in her toes this woman was something else. Her skirt suit was accented with ruffles and patterned in every shade of Gauguin's palette. Her platinum blonde hair was almost entirely covered by a hat so flamboyant she had to duck her head under the doorframe to pass inside the apartment. In that ridiculous get-up, she looked like a cross between Carmen Miranda and a gangster's moll.

The costume quality of this woman's clothing somehow soothed Mirjam. In comparison, the eyelets in her white cotton nightgown seemed considerably less risqué.

With a look of considerable annoyance, the blonde rolled her eyes and set hands on hips. "Do you know how long it took me to find this place?"

Was her voice always so nasal, or only when she was irritated?

"I've been tearing all over this damn city looking for you! I went to your house, but you'd sold it, so I went to your office, but they told me you quit your job! And now here you are, living in a bachelor apartment on the wrong side of the tracks? Mirjam, darling, what's got into you?"

Mirjam clung to the housecoat she hadn't managed to throw over her shoulders. "Who...who are you?"

She tried to place the woman from school days or work days, but how could she have forgotten a woman so brash and buxom?

The woman crossed her arms in front of her big breasts and tapped her toe against the vinyl flooring. "You really don't know me?" she asked, slamming the door closed with her rear. When Mirjam shook her head, the woman took a step closer and said, "It's me—Skyggen!"

Held in place by some supernatural force, Mirjam shook her head.

"Skyggen," the woman repeated. "Your shadow! Didn't you miss me? Don't you dare tell me you didn't miss me. Oh, look who I'm talking to! You probably didn't even notice I was gone." Skyggen's toothy grin made her comments seem more mocking than self-effacing.

"My shadow..." Mirjam uttered.

The puzzle pieces began falling into place, though yet remained unfocused at a distance.

"On holiday you left me. You took the villa across the way."

"Oh, I'd had enough with this trash heap of a city! I wanted to stay in the sun." Skyggen dropped her body into the one chair in front of Mirjam's television. "No offence, honey, but I was sick of being beaten down by your force of will. I wanted to stay, so I stayed."

Mirjam sat on the edge of her bed and gazed at her shadow's manner of dress. "It looks like you've done very well for yourself."

Sticking out her bronzed left hand, Skyggen showed off a rock too big to be real. Though this detached shadow of hers appeared gaudy enough to wear paste, Mirjam had a niggling feeling the diamond was real.

"You're getting married?" Mirjam asked.

Before she'd lost Skyggen, Mirjam would have felt a pang of jealousy at times like these. Was it fair for her shadow to obtain these things Mirjam only coveted? Now, Mirjam dismissed all negative thoughts. She felt numb...and somewhat nauseous.

A nod of affirmation wasn't enough for Skyggen. She had to go on and on about it. "...and this won't be just any old drive-through wedding! We're planning a seven-day celebration for the whole village. Oh, the villagers love him...well, love him and fear him. You should see how they cower. I tell you, we can't walk down the street without being given gifts of all kinds: fruits and gold and chocolates..."

There was an absence at the base of Mirjam's happiness for her shadow. She felt her joy ought to be balanced out by some emotion on the other end of the spectrum. Envy, though sinful, would have brought down her saccharine high.

"That's wonderful," Mirjam replied through gritted teeth. Her jaw seemed to have locked again. She had to massage the pain from her cheeks before saying, "I'm so happy for you. When is the wedding?"

Skyggen grabbed her hands and squeezed. Her eyes glared with such intensity Mirjam feared her for a quick moment. "That's why I've come here, honey. I've felt so guilty for leaving you all alone! I just couldn't go through with this wedding without you by my side. Of course I'll pay your expenses. I mean, look at me! I'm richer than rich!" With a Hollywood kiss for both cheeks, Skyggen brought Mirjam in for an unemotive hug. "You're like a sister to me! How could I get married without you?"

Mirjam wasn't sure how to feel. Even as she boarded the plane, she had a strange feeling about this whole affair. She believed Skyggen was her lost shadow, but she had a suspicion the flashy woman was being less than truthful about something

Onboard, Mirjam's heart swelled when she found herself seated next to a handsome young man. True, her beauty had deteriorated since her shadow split, but certainly she was still capable of flirtation.

He was adorable, this boy with dimples and floppy brown hair. Better yet, he seemed intrigued as Mirjam introduced Skyggen and told him the bizarre story of their separation. "Meanwhile, I had no idea why I felt so weak and incomplete. It all makes sense now, but it was very frightening at the time."

"I imagine so," the boy said, smiling at Mirjam...or was that smile meant for Skyggen?

"Yes," Mirjam went on. "I used to work an executive job in advertising, but after Skyggen left, I couldn't bring myself to do it anymore. All the lies we told! It made me sick—physically. As if a deodorant could make a woman more beautiful, or a beer make a man more attractive! We were brainwashing a nation." She shook her head. "I had to quit."

Skyggen squeezed Mirjam's hand so hard it hurt. "You know," Skyggen said to the boy, "I was the one who got her that job in the first place."

"That's true," Mirjam confessed. "I didn't want to do it, but a little voice in my head persuaded me to lie on my resume. I claimed I had a Master's degree, when in fact I dropped out after my first year of undergrad. That's partly why I quit: I couldn't bear all the lies."

"And ever since, her fortune's dwindled. When I found her, she was living in a ratty old bachelor apartment with barely a stick of furniture in it."

"That's so sad," the boy said.

Did he mean it? Who could tell, with the goo-goo eyes he was making at Skyggen.

The shadow woman noticed the boy's flirtation—that was certain! She leaned her big boobs across Mirjam's lap and patted his thigh. "But I've come back for my little dear," Skyggen said. Despite the plane's subdued lighting, her diamond sparkled like a star as she worked her way up to the brunette boy's crotch. "Now I've got everything in the world, and I'm going to take care of my girl."

The boy wheezed when Skyggen grasped his package. "That's very generous of you," he whispered, looking around at the plane full of sleeping passengers.

"Yes," Skyggen cooed, rubbing his erection through his trousers. "I can be very generous."

Without another word, Skyggen rose to her feet and pulled the boy down the passage by his hard cock. He seemed to go willingly.

With a despairing sigh, Mirjam sat back in her seat and tried to sleep. At least she could look forward to the leisurely village pace and the country's dry heat. A vacation would do her good.

SKYGGEN'S FIANCÉ WASN'T all what Mirjam thought he'd be. Knowing he was rich and powerful, she'd pictured a handsome young fairy tale prince. A surge of *shadenfreude* coursed through her veins when she met the short, husky man. Perhaps in Skyggen's presence, Mirjam's strong emotions were returning to her. She was a *tad* jealous Skyggen would be living in her soon-to-be-husband's veritable castle looking out over the sea.

Rising to greet them, Skyggen's fiancé offered a chivalrous bow. He was a military man, it seemed—his khaki uniform was the giveaway. "Skyggen, my love! I haven't slept a wink since you left."

Pulling her close to his body, he planted a sensuous kiss on her lips. When he let up, she giggled. The military man released her from his arms and she fell to the floor, sighing as he looked to Mirjam. Embers of a deeply-lit fire burned in his eyes. He latched to her gaze and introduced himself. "I am Valon. You must be my Skyggen's shadow."

I must be her shadow?

Mirjam shook her head just as Skyggen burst between the two. "That's right," Skyggen said. "Remember how I explained that Valon thinks it's bad luck for a woman to be without her shadow? Remember I said he wouldn't marry me if my shadow wasn't present at the occasion?"

Skyggen gave a broad smile as Mirjam pronounced a long drawn-out, "No..."

With a loud laugh, Skyggen said to Valon, "Shadows are so forgetful! Excuse us for a moment." Pulling Mirjam past

31

an ensign and into the hallway, she whispered, "All right, so I didn't exactly tell you the truth. Long story short, he thinks you're my shadow. He'd never marry me if he thought I belonged to somebody else."

"Nice foundation to build a marriage on," Mirjam shot back. "You cheat on him, you lie. Skyggen, you are a terrible person!"

"Yes," she hissed, "but it's better to be a terrible person than the world's greatest shadow!"

Mirjam nearly jumped in response to the long-forgotten sensation of adrenaline coursing through her veins. Grabbing Skyggen by the shoulders, Mirjam gave her a good shake. "But you *are* a shadow! I've been dying since you left me, and you don't even care! You don't about anything but yourself."

Mirjam hadn't shouted once in all the time Skyggen had been away. It felt good, but she was so loud about it Valon came running.

"What is going on out here?" he asked through a thick accent.

Grabbing Mirjam by the hair, Skyggen pulled her head back. "She's belligerent!" Skyggen shrieked. "She threatened to convince you I was actually the shadow and she was my mistress. Every word that comes out of her mouth is a lie!"

Skyggen surely could have gone on, but she stopped speaking when Valon untangled her fingers from Mirjam's hair. Glaring at Mirjam with dark but fiery eyes, he wrapped his hand around her arm just above the elbow.

A thrill ran through her.

"Wilful mare," he growled in a voice full of lust. "Let me show you your place."

As Valon dragged Mirjam along the corridor, she realized why he seemed so strangely familiar: she'd seen him on the news back home. Skyggen's Valon was *the* Valon, the overthrown despot living in exile.

This tyrant was the man Skyggen had chosen for husband?

Mirjam examined his square jaw and shimmering black hair as he tossed her inside a bed chamber. Her heart leapt. The room was barely furnished, but there was a bed to cower upon as Valon lingered in the doorway.

Skyggen stood behind him.

Watching the two standing like that, it hit Mirjam that, married to Valon, Skyggen would always live in the shadows. As much as Mirjam wanted to spite the part of herself that had fled, she felt a warm sense of sympathy for Skyggen.

When Valon marched into the room, Mirjam's heart nearly stopped. He tore off his uniform in what seemed like one smooth motion and threw it into the blazing fire. The rising flame was almost as spectacular as his big cock resting on a cushion of black hair and balls. It seemed to both bounce and harden as he strode toward her.

Mirjam's blood pumped fast through her body when he reached down and grabbed the collar of her blouse with both hands. "You planned to tell lies about my Skyggen?"

The fear was more arousing than any pleasure Mirjam had experienced. But she'd be lying to say *yes*, so she said, "No, I wasn't going to lie."

She could see in his eyes what he would do next. And then he did it: he held firm to both sides of her blouse and tore it down the front.

Buttons flew across the room as her breasts swelled.

He grabbed her white lace bra and ripped it from her body. "Tell me the truth," he said, throwing her clothes into the fire.

"I am," Mirjam squealed. She hoped he wouldn't believe her.

And he didn't. His thick fingers tore through her skirt and panties as she looked on in mortified excitement.

"What will you do to me?" she asked.

Her pulse throbbed between her bare legs. She wanted to hear the words.

The expression in Valon's eyes was not that of anger, but of fierce passion. He left Skyggen in the doorway as he flipped Mirjam on to her stomach. Her legs hung off the bed. Her feet planted on the floor. She whipped her head around just in time to catch him thumping his cockhead against her ass cheeks, leaving trails of precum in his wake.

When Mirjam squirmed with wet anticipation, Valon mistook her longing for wilfulness. He grabbed her hips and pressed his fingers so deep into her flesh she knew she'd see bruises later.

"Skyggen," he called. "Get over here and hold your shadow's hands still."

Mirjam put up no fight as Skyggen leaned across the bed to grasp her wrists. She shot Skyggen a crafty smile, as if to say, "Ha! Your man is about to fuck me, and there's nothing you can do but stand by and watch."

But Skyggen didn't seem put off by the situation. Judging by her keen grin, she might even enjoy the spectacle. Perhaps Mirjam had found something she could respect in her shadow: openness to new experiences, a complete lack of jealousy, and the heart to love a tyrant.

Squeezing Mirjam's ass cheeks, Valon slid his thick tip along the wetness of her lower lips. When Mirjam moaned, Skyggen squeezed her hands and released a giggle of affinity. That cock knew what it wanted, and it wanted to pummel her.

He launched himself inside.

His shaft raced through her wet pussy, lodging deep within. He rested for a moment inside her warmth before quickly pulling out. Mirjam sighed when he left her body, and Skyggen threw her face into Mirjam's open hands.

Valon pounded her pussy again, like a rocket straight inside. His cock felt so huge she opened her legs wider. That, Valon took as intention to escape. Wrapping one of his legs around hers, he pressed his heel down on her toes to keep her in place.

"Hold her wrists," he howled to Skyggen.

But Skyggen released Mirjim's wrists and held her hands instead. In a strange sense, Mirjam felt closer to Skyggen now than she'd felt throughout the trip. They were one, were they not? Form and shadow, land and ocean, known and unknown?

Skyggen, that gaudy blonde, was Mirjam's unlived life.

And now, as they held hands on the bed, Mirjam lived that life.

She'd never done this before. Yes, she'd made love, but she'd never been fucked by a stranger—let alone the exiled dictator engaged to her shadow! As Mirjam bucked back against Valon's raging cock, the fire warmed her legs. Valon pummelled her like she knew he would, and Mirjam took it all in. It hurt. It panged against the mystery inside of her, but she loved it. She thumped her ass back against his hairy front.

"Your ass is excited," Valon hissed. "I see your hole pucker and beg."

Mirjam's stomach clenched. She knew what came next, and she recognized its inevitability, but the idea made her cringe. "Please don't hurt me," she yelped.

The statement itself made her skin tingle.

"Don't worry," Skyggen said, petting Mirjam's arm. "It hurts at first, but you'll get over it." When Mirjam pressed her nails into Skyggen's skin, the shadow woman chuckled, "Relax, sweetie. It'll be all right."

Valon pulled his cock from Mirjam's pussy. When he set his tip at the entrance to her asshole, it was still dripping with her juices. Her stomach felt fluttery and her legs went weak, but Skyggen held on tight. Valon reached for her snatch. With two fingers, he brought out more juice and slathered her asshole with the stuff.

She felt slick to the touch.

As he pressed his cockhead past her assring, Mirjam grasped Skyggen's hands. She tried to contain her scream, but she simply couldn't. It hurt. It hurt, but to an acceptable degree, like getting spanked again and again—the site was sore, but it was impossible to stop. She knew, as in all things, if he kept going the pain would subside.

Life was like that.

Her ass blazed as he entered her.

He eased in at first.

Yes, he was forceful, but he wasn't rough about it.

At first.

Once he'd sunk his cock inside her hole to a degree that pleased him, he eased it out again. She clawed at Skyggen's hands, but Skyggen only smiled fondly at the view. Valon pushed his palms flat against Mirjam's ass cheeks before pushing them apart.

She turned her head to see what he was doing. The instant she saw her body in that state, with her cheeks splayed and a firm cock between them, she no longer feared pain. Pain would heal. She wanted that cock inside her ass.

She bucked back as he thrust forward.

"Oh, so you like this, do you?" Valon growled.

His voice was sexy in a reviling sort of way. She wished his voice could fuck her cunt while his cock pelted her ass. Why couldn't she have everything at once? Christ, she didn't even have a shadow anymore—she deserved *something*! But her pussy sat longing while Valon went at her asshole. That empty space ached with jealousy of the crack that was too full, and soon to get fuller.

From the tone of his moans and sensual mutterings, Mirjam could tell Valon was going to come.

Though he was the first actual dictator she'd encountered, she knew his type. He would blow his load, and then pull out, leaving her broken and sore and full of cum. Even so, she'd have a smile on her face. She was smiling now, in fact, through the pain and the hunger.

Skyggen mirrored her expression of sheer joy.

Mirjam screamed in agony and bliss, urging her ass back against Valon's prick as he reamed her. It was horrible and it was so, so good.

She pushed back against him.

He never eased up once he was into his groove. Valon kept at her, pressing his thumbs deep into her ass cheeks while he dug his fingers into her hips.

With an explosion of approval, Valon lifted Mirjam clear off her feet and plunged his cock deep inside her ass.

Clinging to his prick, she shrieked and pressed her eyes tight shut. Held aloft by Valon's strong hands, her feet dangled over the floor. She started to slip. She tried to dig her fingernails deeper into Skyggen's hands, but she somehow lost them. When she opened her eyes, Mirjam found herself clawing at the bedcovers.

Had Skyggen abandoned her? Or was she hiding under the bed?

Setting Mirjam's feet on the floor, Valon pulled out, but he didn't leave. He took a few steps to the side as Mirjam rose upright and gazed across the room. Now she could see. She could see Skyggen's brightly-coloured clothing strewn across the floor on the other side of the bed.

"Look up," Valon said, pointing to the cream plaster. He seemed in awe. "Look at the wall."

As she did, Mirjam realized that, for the first time since she'd come to this country on holiday, she cast a shadow. It wasn't perfectly black, she noticed, but a dusty shade of grey. It was taller than Mirjam, and its reach exceeded her grasp.

"Skyggen," she mouthed. The word was silent.

"So you were telling the truth after all," Valon mused, watching her naked body against the fire. "Skyggen was the liar."

Mirjam reflected for a moment before answering, "I suppose so."

When she spotted Skyggen's eccentric hat on the floor, she was overtaken with glee. Rushing past Valon on the pads of her feet, Mirjam picked it up and set it on her head like a vintage costume. A keen grin broke across her lips as she turned to look at Valon. He'd lost his fiancée to Mirjam. He would need a new one. He'd need a woman who could fill her shoes.

"Well?" Mirjam asked, cocking Skyggen's feathered hat. "What do you think?"

© 2010 Giselle Renarde

To Dream of Her True Love's Face

"Two bay leaves and a sprig of rosemary," her sister whispered, sprinkling the bundle with rosewater. "All that remains is to wrap them in the leaf from a cherry tree and you shall dream of your true love's face."

"And if I dream of Paul," Emma asked doubtfully, "I should accept his proposal of marriage?"

"Well, of course you should, silly girl!" Rosalind tucked the fragrant bundle under Emma's pillow and kissed her forehead. "You must accept his proposal whether or not you dream of him, or risk becoming an old maid like your sister!"

Dear Rosalind chuckled and rose from the bed as Emma pulled her fine Parisian quilt across her chest. "I have my doubts about marriage."

"Nonsense," Rosalind clucked. "You shall dream of Paul's face, and you will know in your heart he is your one true love."

Emma sighed as her sister departed, but perhaps there was some enchantment in her sister's parcel of herbs after all. When Emma's reluctant eyelids weighed heavy and closed shut, she tumbled directly into sleep.

Hooves fell, signaling the advance of a powerful creature.

At once, Emma beheld a proud chestnut horse approaching from a great distance. Even in sleep, its rider stole her breath away. The man on the horse was certainly not Paul, and as she gazed more closely upon his face, Emma realized this was not a man at all! The rider was a woman, neither a dainty Englishwoman in petticoats nor a colonial farmwoman in cotton skirts, but a proud Native warrior dressed all in leather.

The Native woman's face was unlike any Emma had observed in the talented Mr. Catlin's paintings. Her hair was black as a raven's and shimmered bluish against the blinding sunlight. Her copper skin glowed with the radiance of a star, her features noble and well-placed cheeks neither chubby nor gaunt.

As Emma looked on in rapture, a breeze picked up and tossed the woman's long hair over her shoulders. A stronger wind then urged her head to the side until at last she looked directly into Emma's eyes. Her expression hardened, but Emma's fear and excitement and great trepidation spilled into an eager smile. How could she impress her adoration upon this warrior woman? What could she do but grin widely and invitingly?

After a moment that felt to Emma like an eternity, stone melted and the radiant woman offered a glowing smile in return. Even her dark eyes beamed with cosmic light, until Emma blinked from the sheer luminosity. Soon the white light overtook her and she was forced not merely to close her eyes, but to cover them.

When she stole her hands away, Emma was dismayed to see daylight filtering in through the lace curtains of her bedroom window. The dream had gone, and she was alone. Frightfully alone.

Emma dressed into a fine white frock, for she had no maid in this godforsaken "New World" country. She then slipped down the stairs and into her chair at the breakfast table.

"Good morning, dear Sister!" Rosalind squealed. "I suppose visions of Paul have detained you. Will you accept his proposal this morning?"

Despite the shame lingering on her hazy mind, Emma sat up straight in her chair and cracked her egg with firm resolution. "No, Sister, I did not dream of Paul."

Even Father set down his newspaper at this shocking statement.

"Who, then?" Mother asked. "Emma, dear, of whose face did you dream?"

"I..." Emma stared at her egg, with no desire to eat it. She stumbled on her words. "I am not fully certain."

When she told her inquisitive family of her dream, of the horse and its beautiful dark-haired rider dressed all in leather, Father choked on his morning tea. Mother dropped the marmalade knife to her china plate.

After an eternity of silences, Rosalind laughed like a raucous sailor. "Perhaps," she suggested, "the horse is your one true love!"

Mother tittered at the suggestion, and soon Father chuckled along. How Emma wished to join them! How she wished she could laugh at the very possibility of loving a radiant woman rather than a safe young Englishman, but she knew in the depths of her soul she had dreamed of her true love's face, and the family would never, never understand.

Urging her chair back against the polished hardwood, Emma raced from the dining room. The family whispered between themselves as she departed, but in that moment she had little desire to hear the mocking words they spoke. Passing through the kitchen, she grabbed a berry basket. She was expected to offer her answer to Paul today, but how could she very well break the boy's heart? He was a nice enough sort, but he was not her one true love.

In her pretty white frock, Emma tore through the woods with no destination in mind. She wished to be far from town and family. If only she could live here in the forest! Yes, a wild streak ran through her. Emma's mother had always said this was due to her fierce orange hair, and she could feel it now, stronger than ever before.

Clinging to her basket, Emma took dainty steps toward the marsh berries, knowing those most difficult to pluck always tasted sweetest. The delicious red fruit was too far to grasp on reaching, and Emma must walk a little ways out along the beaver dam to fetch it.

When still Emma could not reach the fruit she so desired, she chanced step out onto a patch of marsh. At once, the spongy soil gave way underfoot. Emma plunged into the muddy waters all the way to her pallid breast. In shock, she reached across the useless marsh flowers to steady herself.

"Help!" she cried as muddy water seeped into her white leather boots and soaked her ankles. "Somebody, please help me!"

The marsh water crept up underneath her petticoats until even her undergarments were wetted. Emma grasped the few grasses in her midst to keep afloat. She kicked her feet, but they were caught in the mud at the base of the marsh. It was useless, trying to escape on her own. She needed a savior, and called out as a horse trotted up along the path. When its rider came into view, Emma's heart nearly beat out of her chest. It was none other than the woman from her dream: dark hair and eyes, and a radiant glow emanating from her face and her shoulders.

"You!" Emma cried out, feeling at once relieved and fearful. The vision of this warrior woman brought out a boldness in her that had so long been suppressed. "I dreamed of you. You are my one true love!"

The woman on the horse cocked her head and furrowed her brow. For a moment, Emma wondered if she understood the English language, but the radiant beauty then cackled and said, "Your one true love? I very much doubt it."

Emma blinked forcibly and quickly to ensure she was not dreaming even now, but her dream figure continued to laugh. Why would this stunning woman ridicule her? Emma's godmother was a Duchess, for heaven's sake! Any person, woman or man, should be more than happy to be called Emma's one true love.

Still, the woman's laughter made Emma feel small and silly, and she realized she must offer some form of explanation. "I put a rosemary satchel under my pillow," she said, "and I dreamed of your face."

"Superstition." The woman slid down from her chestnut horse and landed on her feet like a cat. She was very tall, and her long hair glinted in the sunshine as she tossed it behind her shoulders. "If you were indeed my one true love, you would have no trouble escaping this marsh on your own."

"Well, never in my life have I heard such drivel!" Emma replied. When she realized how like her mother she sounded, a hot blush bloomed across her cheeks. "What I mean to say is that I called out and you appeared. Please, you must help me out of this cesspool."

The woman from Emma's dream ran a loving hand down her horse's mane. "If you want my help, you must first help yourself."

Emma kicked her feet out of anger. Her shoes were now caked in mud. How could she possibly be expected to escape with no help?

"I cannot get out on my own," Emma replied.

Her unwilling hero offered only a shrug. "Then I supposed we are at an impasse."

Emma pursed her lips, and then nodded self-righteously. "Yes, I supposed we are."

In silence, the woman clad in leather looked down and smiled. She seemed to derive a twisted sort of satisfaction in watching Emma struggle against the mud and the water plants.

"Yes, what is it?" Emma shouted. "What, pray tell, do you find so vastly amusing?"

"I find it amusing," the woman taunted, "that you have demanded my assistance and informed me that I am your one true love, yet you haven't bothered to ask who I am."

This was absolutely true, but to admit it would only show weakness. "That may be the case, but you have not asked who I am either."

"Who you are is of no consequence to me," the woman replied, her face like stone.

Emma's muscles clenched underwater. What insolence!

"Then why do you stand about watching me struggle?" she demanded, gripping the marsh grasses with her fingers. "Why not get back on your horse and ride away, if you're not going to help me?"

The woman smiled like a vixen. In one cunning leap, she bounded onto her horse and said, "I will do as you say."

Emma bided her time in calling the rider's bluff, but she waited too long. When she called out, "Wait! Please come back. I need you!" the woman of her dream had already disappeared into the woods.

For a time, Emma waited upon the mysterious rider's return. When the stunning horsewoman did not come back immediately, Emma wondered if she hadn't dreamed the entire encounter. Surely her true love would never reject her, and never behave so unpleasantly. Now she clung to surrounding plants and called out, "Help me! Is anybody nearby? I am caught in the marsh. Please do help!"

When she heard the sound of hooves against the forest floor, Emma's heart leaped in her chest. The radiant but mocking woman once again made her way to the clearing, leading behind her a horse stocked with bundles of branches and ferns. Emma's emotion drained away.

"If you would not help me before, I hardly expect you to help me now," Emma grumbled.

The woman grabbed bundle after bundle from her horse's back before sending the mare off to graze. Emma awaited a response as she watched the woman build a fire pit close to the water, but there was none forthcoming.

"My name is Emma. Who are you, if I may be so bold?"

Rising tall beside the fire, the woman dusted pine needles from her knees and stared into the flames. "I was born in the sky," she said, "where I was given the name Star Dancer."

"Star Dancer," Emma repeated, unsure whether the woman was mocking her. *Born in the sky indeed!* Still, she admitted, "That's a lovely name."

"It was more than just a name," Star Dancer went on, absently braiding her long black hair as she gazed into the fire. "I was born to the stars, and I thought I would always live among my kind."

Star Dancer stared for a moment longer before releasing a harsh breath and shaking out her braid. Tramping just beyond the flames, she organized her bundles of branches.

"What are you doing?" Emma asked.

"What does it look like I'm doing?" Star Dancer shot back. "I'm building a shelter."

Emma's heart smiled at the response. "Then you are staying here with me, Star Dancer?"

"Where else am I to stay?" she asked as she threw together a lean-to big enough for the pair of them. "I've been banished from my home and sent down to live here. This is not where I belong, but I am not allowed to return to the sky."

"I suppose, in a broad sense, I have been banished from my home as well," Emma reflected. "I was meant to accept Paul's proposal this morning, but I won't do it."

"Because I am your one true love?" Star Dancer cackled disbelievingly.

Emma closed her eyes and remembered her dream, and then opened her eyes and saw her dream come alive. "Yes," she told Star Dancer. "I dreamed you were coming, and now you are here."

Star Dancer ceased construction for a moment to gaze down at Emma. Though her face was stone, her eyes glittered.

"Why can you not save me?" Emma asked again. She kicked her feet, but could not free herself from the grips of the marsh. How could she be expected to free herself when the mud had very nearly swallowed her whole? With bile in her heart she spat, "It's obvious why you were banished from the sky. You really are a perfectly horrid woman. Why you should be my one true love, I haven't the faintest clue. Perhaps I ought to marry Paul after all!"

But the provocation did nothing to invoke Star Dancer's help, or even her anger. The fallen star only continued to build her new home near the water's edge. She sang quietly to herself as she poked fresh pine boughs into the roof and lined the floor with deep green ferns.

Every moment of Star Dancer's silence brought another droplet of anger to Emma's belly. "Will you please speak to me, you wretched woman?"

Star Dancer only chuckled as she shook her head slowly. "And what would you like me to say?"

Emma had no idea what Star Dancer ought to say. She only knew she didn't care to be ignored. "I knew you must be a star from the moment I first saw you," Emma said, employing her father's method of flattery to secure the upper hand. Of course, in this case she meant what she said. "You have a star's radiance about you. Your skin gleams in the sunlight, and your eyes sparkle so." She sighed. "I do envy you, Star Dancer. How I would love to be a star!"

"I very much doubt it," Star Dancer answered. "You'd have been cast away quick as I was, and for the same cause."

"Oh." Emma hesitated before asking, as delicately as possible, "Did you dream of your true love's face also?"

Star Dancer took a rest from perfecting her shelter, and kneeled down by the fire. With a faint smile, she said, "I thought I knew my true love, but she was the wife of a jealous man. When he discovered our affection, my lover denounced me. She said I'd forced myself upon her, which I swear was not the truth. But none of that matters now. I cannot redeem myself. I'm doomed to live out my years sitting here, watching you fumble about in that marsh."

When she realized Star Dancer was teasing her, Emma laughed. "Well, you realize you could pull me out of this mess. We are castaways both."

Star Dancer's eyes glowed with ephemeral kindness. She smiled, but said, "There is nothing a star can do but cast a light. It is for you to take up that light and make use of it. I cannot rescue you, only inspire you to free yourself."

Though she puzzled it over, Emma could not decipher much meaning from such an obtuse statement. "You are a star, but you have been cast down. Can you not help me as any caring person would?"

The fallen star seemed to reflect on Emma's question as she gazed into the fire. Nodding, Star Dancer then drew herself up and crept across the narrow ledge of the beaver's dam. When she arrived near to Emma, she sank to her knees and leaned far forward. Emma wasn't at all certain what to do until Star Dancer's lips met hers.

The kiss between them seemed to melt the muddy white frock from Emma's body. As Star Dancer's tongue moved in her mouth like a serpent, her mind grew hazy and her body felt light as air. She kicked her feet until they came out of her boots, and lifted up her hands until her frock fell from her arms. Throwing them around Star Dancer's lean but strong shoulders, Emma ran her fingers through the star woman's glassy midnight tresses and kissed her with all the more vigor.

Emma's clothing was caked in mud, and it plunged down into the marsh. Wearing nothing but her once-white undergarments, she clung to Star Dancer's firm body as the star pulled her from the mud.

With care, Star Dancer scooped Emma up and carried her across the dam. Nestled in warm arms and the summer breeze, Emma felt as though she were soaring through clouds. She wrapped her arms around Star Dancer's neck, and when Star Dancer broke their kiss to set her down in the clearing, Emma could only look up in wonderment. She was muddy and nearly nude, but she felt no shame as she gazed upon her true love's face.

"You dirty, filthy woman." Star Dancer chuckled, tracing a finger down Emma's cheek. And then her eyes squinted and an impish smirk broke across her lips.

Summoning her chestnut mare, Star Dancer helped Emma up and then leaped onto the animal herself.

"We need to cleanse you," Star Dancer said, her whispered breath hot on Emma's ear.

As the horse raced across the clearing, Emma clung to its mane. She was accustomed to riding side-saddle, as ladies must, and at once understood why riding like a man had been forbidden to her. Sometimes she thought the world existed solely to deny young women their pleasures. Indeed this ride pleased her like no other, but perhaps that owed to Star Dancer's deft fingers, which fiddled with her corset as they galloped. When the corset ties came loose enough, Star Dancer tore the whalebone implement from Emma's tender frame and tossed it to the wind.

Emma had never felt so free. Placing all her trust in Star Dancer's waiting hands, she threw her arms in the air. "I have found my true love, and she is mine! She is mine!"

Laughing, Star Dancer cupped Emma's breasts. As the mare rode on, those pale mounds bounded and tumbled against Star Dancer's palms. The sensation of rough hands against her untouched flesh sent a queer sensation through Emma's belly. The tingling in her lower regions overwhelmed her, and she made her body heavy against her lover's so Star Dancer would continue to fondle her breasts. When Emma turned her head to beg another kiss, Star Dancer not only complied but also pinched Emma's nipples. A shock like lightning scorched her thighs, and she kissed her love with yet more fervor.

When the mare raced into the lake's clean water, Star Dancer hopped from its back. As Emma slipped down after, Star Dancer tore off her muddy silk pantalettes. Emma looked in all directions, at once alarmed and aroused. Not since she was a very small girl had she been naked out of doors, and even then her mother had scolded her brutally for it. Now there was nobody but Star Dancer to behold her nude body in all its glory. As Emma stood proudly, ankle-deep in the cool lake water, her one true love stripped off leather garments and tossed them onto the beach.

Emma had grown accustomed to her own body's soft pink nipples and pretty bush of orange hair. Star Dancer's nakedness both shocked and awakened her senses. Her true love's skin was more golden-hued than her own, and those nipples darker atop smaller breasts. The triangle of hair between Star Dancer's athletic thighs was a startling black, and it shone in the summer sun.

As the mare sauntered away, Sky Dancer grabbed hold of Emma's shoulders and pressed her down until her knees met the wet sand. Sky Dancer bent and splashed her with cool water until droplets bled down her chest and her nipples hardened into tight pink buds.

"Do you feel dirty now?" Sky Dancer bid as she sank into the lake, splashing her own chest with cool water. "Because, if I am your one true love, I feel it is my duty to rub you clean."

Emma wasn't certain of Sky Dancer's precise meaning, but she did not wish to betray her naïveté. "Please do," she said, leaning back on her elbows and extending her legs.

The ride had made her most sensitive parts all the more tender, and Emma gasped when Sky Dancer slid one leg under her thigh and the other overtop. As the waves lapped the shore, Sky Dancer pressed her body closer inside the V of Emma's thighs and she wasn't sure what this was or how she was expected to reciprocate. When black hair kissed orange Emma jumped, and yet the sensation was so unequivocally pleasurable, she found herself pushing back against Sky Dancer.

There was more wetness between the women than simple lake water. With every kiss of lips on lips, lust mounted in Emma's core. Her breasts swelled and even her heart felt bigger as she pressed her toes into wet sand and moved her hips in circles. Each time she pushed her bottom down into the sand, clear water streamed across her paper-white belly. Every time she raised her hips up to the blue sky, water trickled off. She was hypnotized by the motion of their hips.

Sky Dancer moaned as she moved, and let her head fall back into the lake. When she lifted it up again, water streamed down her nose, dodging her lips before dripping from her chin to her chest. Her beautiful hair ran like black streams down her breasts before joining the motion of her hips.

"Is this new to you?" Sky Dancer asked as she glided her smooth wet lips up and down Emma's.

The answer seemed so obvious that Emma only responded to say, "Everything feels wonderful!" As she spoke, the words became all the more true. Queer sensations rode up her belly, all the way out to her fingertips. Her toes tingled, even as she curled them around wet sand. Something very unusual occurred within her body, and she couldn't deny the pleasure of the experience.

Without quite knowing why, Emma sent her fingers rushing through the hair below her navel, only to curl around Sky Dancer's black bush. Sky Dancer cried out encouragements as she smacked her lower lips—and a tremendous amount of water—against Emma's.

Emma wasn't certain what she was doing. Guided only by lust, she pressed the meat of her palm between her mound and her lover's, stroking back and forth until her flesh felt sizzling hot. Sky Dancer shrieked and covered her face before running long fingers through her wet hair. Emma's muscles ached as she moved with frantic pulsations, but she could not bring herself to stop until they'd climbed the mountain before them. As she bucked her hips in time with Sky Dancer's and rubbed their mounds in a frenzy of passion, she saw them rounding the tip.

They arrived together, and the view from the summit was magnificent.

Everything afterward was a slow tumble through perfection. Sky Dancer climbed up Emma's body and rested her head on Emma's breast as the water lapped against them. Finally Emma interrupted their bliss to beg her way out of the lake. After all, she reasoned, she'd spent more than enough time underwater for one day.

With kindness, Star Dancer helped Emma onto the waiting mare. As they trotted through the clearing, she wrapped her arms around Emma and said, "I searched for my true love among the stars, and I found her stuck in a marsh."

Emma set her sleepy head against Star Dancer's shoulder. "Even if I hadn't dreamed of you last night, I would have known you for my true love the moment we met."

Star Dancer kissed Emma's forehead, holding her close as they approached the place they would henceforth call home. Emma had never imagined living out her days as an inhabitant of the woods, and a lover of the trees and creatures therein. And, yes, a woman's lover too. She adored the star who had brought her to embrace the mud and the mess of nature, as well as the breathtaking beauty of the flowers and the birds. Together, they would grow in love and wisdom.

In town, rumors spread of Emma's "sickness," and her "life of sin" with a Native woman in the forest. After a time, this gossip circulated to those who were needed to know, and each year a few young seekers came out in partners or alone to learn from the wise women of the woods. Though she granted it was no better than a parlor trick, the first gift Emma gave these new friends was a rosemary satchel to dream of their true love's face.

ANGELS AND SHADOWS SEXY SURPRISES

After many long years together, some trying and others joyous, Emma and Star Dancer one night fell asleep before the fire. When they awoke, they were stars in the sky, looking down on the place they'd lived in harmony and taught pride and acceptance to generations of young people. And now, when seekers gaze into the night's darkness, they will see above the marsh a fallen star risen again and hear the laughter of lovers and wise women.

Kandinsky's Shirt Button

A rthur's mother died Tuesday at 7:32pm.

They were all there to see her into the next world, which she didn't believed in anyway. They decided to leave all the sorting through curio cabinets and underwear drawers and piles and piles of junk mail until after the funeral.

The funeral was Saturday at 10am, though to be perfectly accurate it didn't get started until 10:13: the witching hour, according to Judy. Something to do with *The X-Files*. The burial was to follow, of course, and that didn't get underway until 11:27. Much later than anticipated.

Earth to earth, ashes to ashes, dust to dust...

"Are you coming in our car?" Judy asked, stone-faced as she handed Arthur a tissue. "You can go with Nancy instead, if you want. She has room."

"Nancy's patronizing."

"Don't be a pest," Judy scowled, clawing at the tree sap on his lapel.

Arthur brushed her hand away. "*She's* the pest. And those kids of hers irk me."

"Be nice! Those kids are your nephews."

"They're always staring, and if they're not staring they're jumping. It vexes me."

"What's with all the new words, Arthur? You been reading the dictionary again?"

"I didn't get to the library this week."

Knowing his sister was looking at him, Arthur stared down at her feet. Did she realize she'd worn navy shoes with black slacks? Call the fashion police! Major faux pas, and if Arthur noticed everyone must have.

"You okay, Arthur?" Judy finally asked. He knew that was coming.

"Yeah. I'm gonna walk back to Nancy's."

"Walk? It'll take you an hour."

"It's not that far. I just..." A firm grip like the icy hand of death took Arthur's throat in a stranglehold. He waited a moment, still staring at Judy's shoes, to see if it would release his vocal cords and let him say, *I just want to walk*.

Arthur squinted away the tears welling up in his field of vision and they fell into the gravel road of the cemetery.

"You just want to walk," Judy said, always the telepath of the family. She put an arm around his shoulder, offering another tissue as he nodded. "Okay, you walk then. We'll see you at the house."

Most of the cars were already gone. The rest drove by him as he trudged down the path listening to the sound of gravel underfoot, of gravel under tires. Then there was a different sound, the sound of something shifting, something moving through the hedge.

It was a rabbit.

Not a white rabbit –not that kind of rabbit—but a grey hare with wide eyes. When Arthur crept around the side of the hedge to get a better look, the hare was off like a shot towards a row of pine trees near the old stone wall keeping the cemetery from spilling into the outside world. The city can't handle too much death, though God knows it gets enough on the news.

As Arthur tiptoed around the pines, the rabbit got bigger and bigger until it was as big as a woman crouching in the grass. Wait, no, that *was* a woman crouching in the grass. Her long grey coat looked like the rabbit's. Still as can be, her arm was extended toward the hare. In her palm sat an orange.

"Rabbits don't eat oranges," Arthur whispered.

The woman made no response, probably afraid the hare would take flight if she budged even an inch. She was probably right, too.

"They like dandelions," he continued, plucking one from the long grass and settling in beside the woman with hair like a black cat. Or, at least, it would be if cats grew long hair in loose curls.

Maybe it wasn't like a cat at all.

As Arthur crouched beside the woman, her spicy perfume coursed through his body from his nose to his toes. He almost forgot what he was doing when the grey hare snatched the dandelion from his fingers with a violence you'd never expect from a bunny.

Once it had its treat, it took flight along the base of the stone wall until its little legs were long gone.

"Bye bye, bunny," the woman bid, rising to her feet in one graceful stride. Her voice was low and fluttery, like a sultry butterfly.

For the first time, Arthur got a good look at her face. She was beautiful. Her dark eyes were larger even than the frightened rabbit's and they were lined in thick black lashes.

Her lips were full and slightly parted like she might break into song at any moment, a simple country girl from the hillsides of Spain.

Were there hillsides in Spain? Must be. There were hillsides everywhere.

Getting the sense that he'd been staring a little too long, Arthur stumbled around his brain in search of something to say. "I'm Arthur."

"Violette Belfontaine," the woman replied, extending a hand, trapping his, pressing gently on his fingers.

"Do you always do that?" Arthur asked.

"What?"

"Introduce yourself with your first and last names. Usually I would say, 'I'm Arthur' and you would say 'I'm Violet' and that would be that."

"Violette."

Arthur was staring again. Her grey jacket had fallen open and the cleavage it concealed was...well, think Ann-Margaret in *Carnal Knowledge*. But darker. The kind of tits you just want to slide your cock between.

Arthur shook his head. "What did I say?"

"You said 'Violet,' like 'violin.' It's Violette, like 'viola.'"

"Ah." Discomfited by the silence, he blurted, "My mother died Tuesday at 7:32pm."

Violette's eyes softened. "Aw, come here sweety," she offered, pulling him in until his cheek was pressed against the soft cushion of her breast.

As much as he didn't want to, and as much as he tried to stop himself, Arthur wept into that soft pillow of a chest.

Their height differential was a happy coincidence; he'd never been so happy to be a short man. Wrapping his arms around her waist, he let go of the sorrow he'd held in, standing beside his sisters. Crying was a weakness in their family. It simply wasn't done, particularly when something devastating had just happened.

"Thank you," Arthur snivelled, fishing one of Judy's tissues from his jacket pocket. "Very kind of you. Very kind."

"It's hard, I know. Death is hard," the gorgeous woman comforted, guiding him by linked arms over to a tower of a gravestone. Upon it she set the orange she'd offered to the rabbit. The stone had the name LIM at the top and a sepia photograph of a man on a ceramic oval. The rest of the characters were in Chinese.

"Your... father?" Arthur asked, knowing that must not be right. Violette didn't look Chinese.

"A client," she replied, kissing her fingers and pressing them to the ceramic photograph.

Nodding in response, Arthur raised his eyes to the sculpture of an angel on top of the stone. It was an oddity in this section of the cemetery. None of the other Chinese graves had angel sculptures. Wait, no, it wasn't an angel at all. No wings. It looked like a mermaid. A mermaid? Yes, a mermaid with a cherub at her feet, standing in an overturned seashell. "Why a mermaid?"

"What?"

"Why does your client have a mermaid on his grave?"

Violette furrowed her brow. Her voice was not so soft when she said, "It isn't a mermaid. Mermaids have tails. Does she have a tail?"

"Yes, it's right there."

Exhaling through her nose, the beautiful woman said, "No, that's her dress."

"Maybe it's not a dress. Maybe it's a tail."

"It's a dress."

"How do you know it's a dress?" Arthur challenged.

"Because I designed it. It's Venus. It's the birth of Venus."

"Oh," Arthur squeaked. Clearing his throat to get his voice back down to the right octave, he asked, "If she's being born, why is she wearing a dress? People aren't born wearing clothes."

"I don't know," Violette sighed, shaking her head.

"And is that cupid at her feet?"

The woman's dark eyes sparkled. "Yes! Cupid is Venus' son. He's part of the whole symbolic Venus package; having him in the picture offers further proof that you're looking at Venus."

"Right..." Arthur began. "But, see, if she's only just being born herself, how could already have a son? Were she and her son born at the same time? It doesn't make sense."

Violette's glare was as predictable as it was familiar. Arthur had a knack for pissing people off. It's because he always had to point out the flaws in their statements. Most people didn't think through what they were saying, or doing for that matter. They said things that made no sense. Arthur liked for everything to make sense; it helped to keep the world in perspective.

"You're right," Violette agreed. She was laughing. Just look at that! She'd gone from glaring to giggling. "It's hundreds of years of artistic tradition and it doesn't make any sense at all."

Arthur chuckled along, though the idea of hundreds of years of art that made no sense had his stomach in knots. "An artist, then?"

"No, he was high up in the telecom trade," Violette replied, patting the orange like a child's head.

"I actually meant you. *You're* an artist, I'm guessing."

"Oh," Violette tittered, tossing her head back and shaking out her hair in such a way that her whole body swivelled. "Goodness, no."

"But you designed this sculpture. Aside from making no sense, it really is very lovely."

"Thank you."

"Well, in my book that makes you an artist," Arthur assured her, daring to touch his fingers to the cuff of her jacket.

Violette didn't seem to notice. "You are what you sell. I don't sell my art."

"What do you sell?"

"My soul."

"Well, who doesn't?" Arthur chuckled, removing his fingers from her wrist.

"Fine. My heart, then."

"Your heart?"

"It comes along with my body; a two-for-one sort of deal."

That icy death grip had his heart now, grasping tighter as the words made more and more sense.

"Excellent," Arthur said, though he wasn't sure why. Was it excellent? Was it even a little way down the road to excellent? This woman was beautiful and well put-together, nice clothes, obviously knew a thing or two about art...No, that didn't seem excellent at all.

"I don't work much with smaller clients anymore," Violette declared, digging through her purse for a business card. Her gaze bolted up from her purse to Arthur. "Sorry, I didn't mean small as in small in stature, just small as in short-term. God, I'm an embarrassment, aren't I?"

"Short-term," Arthur repeated, though it came across as a question.

"Long-term contracts are best. Well, they're not really contracts, not in a business sense, at least. More like relationships. I have a great affection for my men, and I'm very selective these days. And yes, I know, people are always arguing with me, 'How can you call it a relationship if it isn't exclusive? How can you call it a relationship when he's paying you?' But my argument has always been, 'Well, isn't that what marriage is?' Maybe not so much anymore, but historically the only reason for women to marry the dreadful men they were set up with was the financial angle. Anyway, I'm an entrepreneur and I make very good money with very little overhead."

"I guess so," Arthur agreed, struggling to keep up. "But what about the whole exclusivity thing?"

"It's the nature of the trade. My men are aware there are others; it's no secret. The key is to make each client feel like he's the only man in the world when he's with me. It's all about feeling special. We all want to feel special."

"Yes, well, what I actually meant was..." He cleared his throat. "Doesn't it bother you that they're not seeing you exclusively? I mean, they're probably not."

Violette's smile fell, the blood draining from her cheerful expression. "It's business," she snapped. "What do I care?"

"Well, you said what you're selling is your heart..."

"Don't split hairs."

"Sorry. That's what I do."

"Don't. Anyway, good old Henry Lim here left me a generous stipend so, as I said, I don't have to work much anymore. His family tried its damnedest to challenge the will, but we go way back, Henry and I. He was my first, actually. Everything just clicked. The whole arrangement worked so well that..."

She drifted, tapping the orange offering with the business card in her hand.

"Now, I'm not saying I haven't taken the good with the bad," she went on. "God knows I have, but I've learned over the years to weed out the ones who are likely to cause me grief. There's always an element of risk in business, but..."

Violette drifted again.

"His daughters still throw away my oranges. Maybe I would do the same. Who knows? Anyway, if you think you may require my services please let me know."

Violette's business card listed her name, cell number and e-mail address. "What's your job title?" Arthur had to ask.

Cocking her head to one side like a vixen, she spoke in a breathy hush. "Let's say, *Paid Companion*."

HER BUSINESS CARD SAT on Arthur's bedside table for eight days, fourteen hours and twelve minutes. She was a whore and he couldn't stop thinking about her! No, not a whore, a *paid companion*. It was her company, her intellect and affection, one paid so handsomely for; the body was just frosting.

But that body... oh, that body!

Violette had written in a special rate just for him on the flip side and, with that, he was able to calculate how many dates they could enjoy without bankrupting him.

Arthur picked up the phone, set it back down. He picked it up and stared at his reflection in the plastic face.

He made a deal with himself: if he didn't dial now, he would shred the card.

The numbers flowed from his fingers into the phone at the thought of never seeing Violette again. There was something so refreshing about her, an uncommon kind of freedom, an unusual outlook. And her creative bent would certainly benefit...

"Violette Belfontaine."

Arthur almost stopped breathing. "So you *do* always do that..."

A giggle of recognition sparkled across the line. "Arthur! I'm so glad you called. How are you?"

"I... uh... I..."

"Your mother's wake went as well as could be hoped? Have you started in on the house-clearing? How are you coping, darling?"

Arthur could hardly find words to stumble over. She remembered him! She, the striking Violette, remembered him, the insignificant spec of an Arthur.

And not only did she remember him, she remembered the things he'd told her that one and only time they'd spoken. Even his coworkers, the people he worked with every single day, forgot to get him a sympathy card. Either they forgot or they just didn't care.

Nobody cared.

Violette cared.

A gush of warmth flowed to where his heart must be until that tender sensation turned into words. "I'm so happy to hear your voice!"

"I feel the same way, Arthur. Now, are you calling to book an appointment, sweety?"

"Yes!" he nearly shouted, like the offer might expire if he didn't get the word out fast enough. "I want to take you out for dinner. Please let me. Will you let me?"

Her deep gurgle of a laugh painted his mind a shade of ease. "Of course, Arthur."

"I love the way you say my name."

"I know, Arthur."

Of course, he had to try on each of his four suits before settling on the black one. Violette had already seen him in it, which made the outfit lucky, somehow. And, this way, if she didn't seem to like him as much as before he would know it was because of some character flaw, not his clothes. It occurred to him, as he entered the dining room at the Windsor Arms, that he hadn't factored the expense of wining and dining Violette into the overall cost of seeing her: a fatal oversight.

She was seated at a private table behind thick velvet curtains. The handful of roses he brought paled in comparison to the commanding beauty of Violette. A silk damask gown in a subdued shade of gold caressed her curves as she rose to greet him with a peck on the cheek. "So lovely to see you, Arthur! Are those for me? You shouldn't have!"

"Oh, yes, right. Forgot I was holding them," he stammered, handing the roses to his beautiful date. "You look..."

A server came up behind him, setting a platter of grilled flat breads with artichokes, tomatoes and various dips down beside Violette's half-empty glass of white wine. "I hope you don't mind that I've ordered a starter; I'm absolutely famished and craving hummus. Why are you still standing? Come, sit beside me," she bid, sliding to the far end of the upholstered bench.

"Beside you?"

"Why not?"

"Good point," Arthur shrugged, plopping himself in beside her.

Violette's whole body curved toward him like a sunflower drawn to that vast orb of fire around which the planets spun. It took nothing more than the sense of omnipotence she cast upon him to get Arthur hard as Brazil nut.

Through the slit down the front of Violette's gown poked the most sensual thigh he'd ever seen. It would have taken him all the strength in the world to keep from touching it if Violette hadn't grabbed his hand and set it against that softer-than-soft flesh.

When she pressed on his fingers, encouraging a rough squeeze, Arthur's cock strained in his trousers, pumping precum into his jockeys. Without meaning to, he released a pleasured moan, quickly covering his mouth with both hands.

Violette gurgled that deep breathy laugh as she dipped a triangle of flatbread into the hummus. Topping it with a piece of marinated artichoke, she popped it in her mouth. Her perfect dark lips shimmered with olive oil from the bread. She made a noise, an *mmm* sound as she chewed.

The words gushed again from his swollen heart: "God, you're beautiful."

Covering her mouth with the back of her hand, Violette issued something that might have been a sneeze or a cough, but was probably a laugh. Swallowing the hummus, she replied, "About as beautiful as Kandinsky's shirt button!"

Arthur chuckled nervously, dunking some flatbread into the orange dip. He wasn't following, but didn't want to reveal his ignorance. Violette took a quick sip of wine before sending her hand on an arousing trip around his thigh. Sweeping her fingers like feathers in his lap, she dusted them across his straining cock. He tried his damnedest not to budge. Any motion, anything at all, might set him off.

"Do you know the artist Wassily Kandinsky?" she asked, tracing light fingers around his throbbing cockhead.

"Not personally," Arthur gasped.

"Of course not—he died in the 40's—but Kandinsky was around for the birth of abstract expressionism. He was interested in the spirit of art, in the spirituality of it." When she took his cock in her firm grasp, Arthur nearly jumped out of his skin. Stroking it overtop his best pants, she went on to say, "Kandinsky believed that everything in our world has a secret soul which is silent more often than it speaks."

"That's beautiful," Arthur wheezed.

Violette popped two cherry tomatoes in her mouth before unlatching his belt and sliding down the fly. Slipping her hand against his gasping flesh, she fondled the hair down there as his abdomen hopped with pleasure. "It's a beautiful sentiment, but he was writing about a shirt button in a puddle."

"Why?" he asked. Or maybe he said 'what' or 'wow;' he really wasn't sure of anything. He wasn't even sure this was really happening. Was this gorgeous woman really fondling his balls? Sculpting his cock like clay? Exposing him to the open air of one of the city's classiest restaurants? If all this was real, it was money well spent.

"He saw this button in a puddle one day, just a run-of-the-mill white men's shirt button. You know the type that are sort of pearlescent? One of those. In the sunlight after the rainfall, this little white button was sparkling like an oyster shell and Kandinsky couldn't help but stop and stare. He was fixated on this gleaming little button in a puddle."

Arthur released a low moan from the back of his throat, though he didn't intend to. Violette wrapped her fist around his cock, pumping the shaft with expert conviction. With every push and pull motion, the muscles in her arms heaved with exertion.

"Anyway," she continued, "that's what inspired Kandinsky's concept of the secret soul. He felt this little white shirt button was communing with him, somehow. It was as if this tiny, mundane thing was glowing with a secret beauty the world could only see if it was really willing to look."

Crossing one arm over the other, Violette grabbed a triangle of flatbread, but spilled most of the hummus down her front. In such a low-cut dress, her clothes were unscathed but a nice drizzle of dip trickled down her breast, which heaved the harder she pumped his cock.

"Oops!" Violette gurgled. "Do you want to get that?

Arthur didn't need to be asked twice. His face nearly fell into Violette's cleavage, tongue drawn as though by gravity to that pert flesh doused in hummus.

As he licked the garlic and chickpea spread from Violette's olive skin, that familiar sensation set in.

He licked again. Licked, lapped, lunched along the cleave of those magnificent breasts. His balls began to quake. His ass cheeks clenched as Violette spread a palm across his cockhead, smoothing it in quick circular motions while she jerked hard on the shaft.

That was about all this man could take. He came before he knew it, before he could stop his head from spinning, before he could stifle the pleasured yelp that left his throat like Icarus launching himself at the sun. In broad strokes, she painted his exhausted cock with cum until he felt every bit the dirty boy.

"I don't really buy it, though," Violette declared, wiping her hands on a white cloth napkin.

"Huh?"

"That Kandinsky's shirt button had a secret soul it was sharing with him and only him. I think he was looking so hard for beauty in random objects that he was bound to find it. That shirt button was beautiful to him because he wanted it to be."

Hazy, Arthur asked, "How did we get onto this topic, again?"

"You told me I was beautiful and I said, 'About as beautiful as Kandinsky's shirt button.' Are you hungry? I could go for steak and frites."

"Yeah, that sounds..."

"Two," Violette told somebody, sticking her head out the velvet curtain.

He would have to try not to fall asleep face down in his dinner. No wine tonight.

ARTHUR WAS QUIET THROUGH dinner, but he could hardly be blamed for his sleepiness following the first orgasm he'd experienced at the hands of a woman since March 20th, 1993. She was astonishing, this Violette. The brains in that girl's head! Amazing. She could be anything. Why was she... why was she what she was? Puzzling. Maybe one day he would feel close enough that he could ask her. Although, he could only take so many dinner bills like tonight's.

"Shall I see you home?" Arthur offered.

Damn. He hadn't factored in the cab fare, and you could hardly take a girl like Violette home on the subway.

"I expect it," she replied with a smile and a playful pinch to his side. Arthur giggled like the Pillsbury Doughboy. "Come on, the loft is just down the street. Keep up!" Umbrella-less in the pouring rain, Violette leapt out from under the Windsor Arms' overhang and sprinted off down the street.

Rejuvenated by the cold rain running streams through his hair, Arthur arrived home with Violette a new man. "The Loft," as she called it, was a tremendous space with ceilings so high it seemed it would take five of him standing on top of one another just to reach the glittering chandelier overhead.

From it to the four corners of the vast room was strung sheer white fabric, giving the space an ethereal glow. The rough wooden boards of the floor were earth and those gauzy reams the heavens above. But what sat between the ceiling and the floors, propped against invisible walls, was by far the most striking aspect of Violette's space.

There were massive canvases everywhere, one supported by another, creating layered walls of art against the old factory windows. A theme became immediately apparent: Venus, the goddess of love. Every canvas was Venus in some form, every painting in a different style: Old Masters, Abstract-Expressionism, Japanese Woodblock, Synthetic Cubism, Impressionism, Byzantine, Pop Art, Fauvism, African Carvings, Pre-Raphaelite, Neo-classicism, it was all there.

"Where did you get all these?" Arthur gushed, approaching a giant reproduction of *The Rokeby Venus*, except the mirror in this one reflected more than just a pretty face. "I've never seen anything so..."

"Don't touch!" Violette cried, running to him in wet heels. Too late. Royal blue paint coated Arthur's fingers, screaming that the artist was in this very room.

"Sorry," Arthur offered, though it was little consolation after ruining someone's painting.

Violette stood staring at the canvas, her expression unreadable. She could have been angry or accepting; impossible to say. From the floor, she grabbed a brush and a palette heaped with dried oils, and some fresh ones.

"I'm always doing thing like this," Arthur stammered. "Can't seem to help making a mess of things."

In three strokes, Violette repaired the injury. "There," she sighed. "No harm done. Feel better now?"

She gave him a peck on the cheek.

"Much," Arthur replied, glowing brighter than the chandelier above Violette's wrought iron canopy. "But you can't have painted all these canvases? There are so many of them and they're all different styles..."

"Maybe I'm all different people," she smiled, wiping her brush down with taltine. "Oh, shoot!"

"What's wrong?"

"I got paint on my dress. Shoot!" she repeated, licking her finger and rubbing it against the golden damask. With a sly smirk, she added, "Guess I'd better go take it off before the stain sets in."

"Guess so," Arthur replied with a throaty laugh that came out sounding far more perverted than he'd intended. He cleared his throat to cover it as Violette slipped behind one of the folding screens carved with birds and Chinese writing.

The silk damask dress flew into the air. She was trying to toss it on top of the pile of clothes already perched on the screen, but it fell right back down, bringing a landslide of dresses cascading with it.

"Shoot."

"Why Venus?" Arthur asked so Violette wouldn't be embarrassed by the sounds of her shuffling clothes and cracking joints.

"Goddess of Love? Venus is my ideal. Or my idol. I'm not sure which."

"Maybe both."

"Maybe. Anyway, every painting is an offering to the spirit of perfect love in the female form, and my home is an altar to that love. It's my form of worship. It's one form, at least..."

Arthur couldn't remember what he was about to say when Violette stepped out from behind the screen guised in a sparkling black number, sheer as the fabric hanging from the chandelier.

Trying not to stare, since it was rude to stare at a woman's body, he focussed on the slippers she wore with feathery little pom-poms at the toes. Of course, his gaze strayed up and up along the borders of the shimmering fabric pooling at her ankles. He skipped by the abyss of her black panties, not nearly brave enough to imagine what lied beneath. Travelling up the firm flesh of her abdomen, he soon arrived at those mountains of soft glowing flesh held firmly in place by the low-cut top of her empire waist peignoir.

One rhinestone button in the shape of a flower maintained its desperate struggle to keep her garment shut when her generous breasts wanted so badly to escape the stranglehold of clothing.

"You love my breasts," Violette observed.

"I..."

"You can't stop staring at them."

"I..."

"You want to lay me down on the bed right now, slip your cock between them and fuck my tits 'til you come all over me."

"I... well, no, I don't want to do that," Arthur stated.

"You don't?" Violette asked with mild surprise, or perhaps amusement, bringing a smile to her face. She took a few steps toward him, slipping her fingers against his wrist under the cuff of his shirt. "What do you want?"

"Well, you were very close, in fact," Arthur replied, the testosterone pumping through his veins encouraging a certain confidence. "Very close indeed, but what I would really like is for you to descend to your knees, if you please."

"Why certainly," Violette responded, slipping to the floor with the grace of a princess. Their height differential would pay off once again. When she tore his belt from their loops, Arthur kicked off his pants and boxers almost before they'd dropped to the floor.

Violette cupped his balls, applying gentle pressure as he fumbled with the bottom few buttons of his white dress shirt, giving up on the rest. Her hands were soft, warm, welcoming, even familiar after their restaurant encounter.

"Would you kindly lean back a little?" Arthur requested. When Violette arched her back, dropping her hands to her ankles, her gorgeous breasts aligned perfectly with his rigid cock.

As he hovered over her soft body, Arthur's cockhead dripped two pearls of precum on to Violette's precious breast.

Balancing awkwardly on one hand, she unclasped the rhinestone button and those tits came pouring out at him, bouncing like jello.

"Grab that bottle?" Violette encouraged, nodding toward the indiscreet industrial-sized container of lube on the bed.

While she held her luscious tits side by side, he drizzled her cleavage with the slippery clear liquid. His cock pounced, striking its head against a dark nipple, when Violette slid her fingers through the trail of lube running down her belly.

Taking his hard body in hand, she pumped the shaft a few times before leaning back to offer her tits to him. He graciously accepted the gift, running his hands across her breasts like a seasoned masseuse. Her flesh was firm, but warm as a ripe strawberry in the summer sun. Across her shining honey-brown skin, Arthur brushed his cock, slick with lube. That sensation of flesh on flesh made his balls quake.

As Violette leaned back, hands on ankles, Arthur's body rattled at the inevitability of reaming those gorgeous tits. He took them in his grasp. They were soft, they were firm. He pressed them together until they buried his cock, until it was lost, enveloped in their incredible warmth.

Moulding those beautiful breasts, he moved between them, thrust in the cleave. What in the world could be better than this? His whole body flowed with Violette's warmth, a tenderness aroused by her satin skin.

She leaned further back and he was on top of her, his legs all around her, his balls brushing her chest as he held fast to those big tits and just fucked the hell out of them. He thrust faster and faster, until he couldn't move as fast as he wanted the friction to feel. That's when he started pulling her slippery tits against him as he thrust, pushing them away as he retreated. Over and over again he manipulated her breasts, Violette squealing as he pressed her dark nipples between his thumbs and forefingers.

There was a quaking in his body, a feeling like gritted teeth, and he was suddenly enraptured. Beyond that. His thighs shook, his back arched and his whole body clenched as the cum soared out.

All he could see were the rainbows of light sparkling from above. Venus, Venus everywhere, and a bed under a crystal chandelier.

From his orgasmic throat fled the words, "Thank you," as Arthur's exhausted legs gave out beneath him. A wooden floor had never been so enticing a place to nap. His eyes were closed and Violette was on top of him, resting with breasts around his sleeping cock and black hair cascading along his side. This was, perhaps, the first time in his adult life Arthur felt utterly content.

ARTHUR AWOKE WITH THOSE same sparkling rainbows of light caressing his field of vision. As much as he wished to get up and use the bathroom, he wouldn't dream of disturbing Violette's slumber.

Back to the Venuses, which he hadn't truly taken in before. Of course, he was seeing them upside down from his position on the floor, but they were striking nonetheless. The huge Picasso-style Venus was probably the most eye-catching, with its bright yellows and greens and its eyes and breasts in all the wrong places.

The allegorical Venus with Mannerist lines was certainly the most thought-provoking. He would have to ask Violette about the meaning of all those queer symbols.

Ah, Violette. Beautiful Violette, so much more than she seemed. When he petted her dark hair, she stirred, emitting that gurgle of a laugh as she wiped a puddle of drool from his skin. Chin resting against his chest, she gazed up at him with messy hair and playful eyes.

"I hate to move, but I really ought to see my way to the little boys' room," Arthur said with deep regret.

"Just through there."

Everything about Violette was precious now. He couldn't leave that tiny space without playing with her soap, smelling her shampoo, checking out her many prescriptions, tasting her toothpaste, dabbing her perfume against his wrist. Every mundane brand in her medicine cabinet was now infused with a special personality.

When he returned to the loft, Violette was huddled like a bunny in centre of her bed. She was perfect. Perfect. She shouldn't be doing this sort of work. Who were these other clients? They couldn't possibly feel the way he did about her.

"Why don't you sell your art?" Arthur suggested. It seemed like the obvious thing to do. "This one here would bring in... oh, I don't know, but a tidy sum. You could earn enough to live for years and keep painting without having to..."

"I would never sell my paintings," Violette stated, face like dark marble.

"But they're beautiful!"

"Exactly! That's exactly it. They're beautiful and they're mine and I want to keep them. What else do I have that's as beautiful as my art?"

"You have you!"

She smiled as though the idea distressed her. "Please don't tell me I'm beautiful. I just can't hear it anymore. My art is what's beautiful and it's all I have. Why can't one thing, just one thing in the world, be mine to keep?"

After a moment in the stillness of blank contemplation, Arthur offered, "You could have me. I may not be beautiful, but I could be yours to keep. If you want."

"My, my! Don't we form quick attachments?" Violette accused, unclasping the rhinestone button on her shimmering peignoir. "You don't even know the real me."

"You're a beautiful person. That's all I need to know."

"Beautiful?" she asked, melancholy. Shadows streaking her face, she rose from the gauzy white bed like a dark water nymph. "You call this beautiful?"

Towering over him, Violette slipped the shimmering peignoir from her shoulders. It fell without a rustle to the wooden floor as she stepped out of her black panties. Arthur averted his eyes. It was rude to stare at a woman's penis. Violette took hold of the unsuspecting organ surrounded in finely manicured black hair. "This body is beautiful to you?" she demanded in a defeated whimper. "Well? Is it?"

That was the moment of knowing, after eleven days, nine hours and three minutes of not knowing. Arthur's mind was a beehive, buzzing with tender numbness. He was warm all over. Hot. Warm. Cold. A heat wave gushed through his veins, making his whole body tremble in mock-disbelief. After all, how could the disbelief be real when this body was just how he'd envisioned it? She didn't need to say. She didn't even need to allude to it, let alone show him. Arthur knew, and his heart glowed with affection for the beautiful, beautiful Violette.

"Yes!" he cried, rushing over to her until he was somehow, miraculously, in her arms and kissing her lips. "Your body is beautiful; it's you!"

"Please stop saying that," she demurred, releasing herself from his grasp and slipping over to the bed. There, she fell face-first onto the mattress, perfect round ass cheeks flying high in the air. "Here," she said, tossing him a condom. "Fuck me. That's what you're paying for."

"Don't be vulgar," Arthur rebuked, picking the condom off the floor. "I'm paying for your company. I'm paying because it's an honour to spent time in your magnificent presence. I wouldn't pay your rates just for sex."

Turning her head, Violette beckoned him, drawing compliments from his mouth.

"Do you really think men would pay so much just for your ass? I mean, it's a lovely ass, certainly, but it's more about you. For me, at least. It's about being around you, it's about the way you make me feel. Happy. You make me happy."

She stared at him, wide-eyed as the grey hare, before repeating, "You don't even know me."

"I'll get to know you. Marry me, Violette. Will you marry me?"

Grabbing a pillow, she pressed her face into the down and laughed. Mockingly or joyfully? Arthur couldn't be sure.

"You're the first to ask," she demurred, sitting up in the bed with legs wrapped around the pillow.

"And I'm the first you'll answer with a yes. Please, Violette. Say yes. Just say yes!"

"Arthur," she replied, shaking her head tenderly. "You want a real woman for a wife."

"You are a real woman. Anyway, there's always the money from my inheritance..."

Hopping from the bed, she walked to him in black slippers, sad eyes beseeching him to stop all this nonsense. "You're a sweet man, Arthur. You deserve better."

"There is no one better!"

"You deserve a Venus."

"You are a Venus!"

"A Venus with a penis?" she spat with an uncharacteristically harsh laugh.

He couldn't bring himself to chuckle in response. "Yes, fine. That's fine. However you are now is fine because I fell in love with you just as you are and I would be happy--no, delighted, overjoyed--to build a home with you in any body. That's not important, Violette. It's *you* that's important. You are the most beautiful, stunning creature I've ever laid eyes on. Well, laid anything on."

"I am not beautiful," she stated, more forcefully than before. "Why do you keep saying that? You're just seeing what you want to see. You're seeing the cloak I'm wearing to disguise the hideousness inside. I'm horrid, Arthur. You're dear and sweet and lovely and I'm just horrid."

"No, you're not seeing yourself properly."

"No, *you're* not seeing *me* properly! Arthur, you are the very embodiment of the anima complex. You're textbook! If anyone were listening to this conversation, they'd be laughing right now."

"I can't imagine what you mean."

"You poor, dear man, chasing some shimmering gossamer dream you've wrapped around a whore. That's all I am. Just a whore. All these paintings of Venus are my aspiration, they're not me. What woman, could ever be a goddess? We are human. We live on earth, in the blood and mud and shit of this planet. To see myself as above all that would indicate an ego inflated beyond all reason. That's how you see me, though: shimmering gossamer goddess."

"How can I see you that way when I don't even know what you're talking about? You *are* beautiful. You're *not* a whore. Don't confuse things. You're mixing things up, you're messing them up. You know I like things organized. You're not a whore! Don't denigrate yourself. You could be anything."

Throwing her dark hair back, Violette cackled, "You think I do this work because I have no choice? Listen to me, Arthur, I have choices and this is the choice I've made. I am an oddity and I intrigue men like you. There was a time when I was getting my little brains fucked out for free, but why not make a business out of what you love to do? I love getting fucked and I do it for money. This is how I want to live and all the concern you show for me won't change that."

Arthur's temperature was on the rise. Arthur's cock was on the rise. "You love getting fucked, do you?" He was on the prowl, hunting her down as she backed onto the bed, grabbing the big bottle of lube.

"I love getting fucked by you."

Even if it was just a platitude, Arthur's heart softened while his cock remained hard. "You love it?" he growled, feeling somewhat estranged from himself in this role of the muscular male, like he was watching himself in a dream.

"I love it," Violette purred, helping him with the condom wrapper.

She slid on the sheath, grasping his cock as she coated it with lube. One leg over his shoulder, she rubbed more lube against her rosebud anus, writhing with pleasure at the sensation. Her experience of self-gratification compounded Arthur's desire for her. The luscious purse of her red lips as she ran her tongue across them was more than he could handle.

Pulling her in by the thighs, he set his cockhead up against her undulating asshole. The slippery ring seemed to be grasping for him, pulling, bidding entry. He pushed, forced his way into that tight hole. The warmth of her body sent shivers through his legs and down his arms, causing him to squeeze her thighs with his fingers as she wrapped her ankles around his neck.

Violette gurgled a moan, tossing her head to one side, and he couldn't resist latching onto her surging breasts. Every squeeze of those dark nipples had a domino effect, making her clench her assring like a vice around his cock. There were moments when she was so tight he could barely move in her and she just milked his shaft with those writhing ass muscles. She was just so beautiful, just so beautiful. That open mouth, those lips pronouncing words of encouragement, the eyes rolling back like the pleasure was too, too much.

It wasn't long before Arthur's thighs were shuddering and shaking for the third time that night. The feeling of coming in Violette's ass was an all-at-once sensation. It snuck up on him, and suddenly he was in the midst of a screaming orgasm without having seen its approach.

Eyes closed, he clenched every muscle in his body as every ounce of energy left him through that one small hole in his straining cock.

On the verge of collapse, he traced his finger through the trail of cum down Violette's front as she hollered down from the heights of ecstasy.

"I'm a sympathetic orgasmic," she smirked.

WHEN ARTHUR AWOKE IN that gauzy white bed under the massive chandelier, the blue light of early morning snuck in between the walls of canvasses. For a long while, he didn't move.

Fearing Violette would wake up if he so much as looked at her, Arthur stared once again at the rows and stacks of Venuses watching over their slumber. When Violette finally did stir, he lay very still.

"Did you enjoy yourself last night?" she inquired.

"Very much so. Very much so." He wasn't quite sure how to broach the subject, so he just spit the words out. "You've got painting to do, I'm sure. I suppose I should pay you and be on my way."

Tossing her hair about, she replied, "Well, I'm not free, Arthur. I'll never be free." Violette stopped shaking her head, as if hit by the double meaning of her words.

"Free from what?" Arthur asked.

"That's not what I meant," she assured him.

"But it's what you said."

"That's not what I mean," she repeated, running her fingers across the gauzy bedding.

Richer for the experience, if poorer of pocket, Arthur stepped onto the street outside Violette's loft. The city, still shaking off last night's storm, sparkled shades of yellow and blue in the early light of dawn.

He stood there for a moment, taking in the earthy-fishy scent of the rainfall and absorbing the feel of a city with no one in it.

There, on the gritty morning-after sidewalk, lived a puddle of rainwater. There in the puddle sat a white men's shirt button, radiant as a pearl in the early morning sun.

© 2008 Giselle Renarde

84

Shadow People

It's not like she could refuse the assignment.

Every quarter, when the new list of investigation sites was posted, Anna drooled over all the incredible projects handed to Sigrid, Jean-Frances, and Dandruff Dan. They'd been at the Institute for years. Her boss, Chief Investigator Gentle Geoff, figured they were more capable of ghost tracking the major hauntings. Did youthful ambition count for nothing in parapsychological academia?

Apparently not.

Searching through the crappy assignments doled out to untenured staffers, she finally found what she was looking for: Anna Fairclaw—her family name was always misspelled on these lists—right next to a project at the very summit of randomness.

"Shadow People? What the hell are Shadow People?" she asked Sulky Sully.

"Why don't you read the descriptor?" he scoffed. As far as she could tell, he'd never stopped resenting her. Before Anna arrived at the Institute, Sully had his own desk, not to mention his own office. Now they shared.

"The Shadow People, or Tarriaksuit as they are known..."

"Read in your head," Sully interrupted.

Anna batted her lashes then bobbed her head like a sardonic *I Dream of Jeanie.* "Yes, master."

The Shadow People, or Tarriaksuit as they are known to the Inuit, are elemental beings described in the mythological systems of the Canadian North. Shadow People are commonly believed to inhabit a world parallel to ours, existing beyond the realm of human sense perception. Disembodied speaking or laughing are often attributed to these beings, as are sounds of footsteps in the distance.

Historically, only the most intuitive residents of the North have felt the presence of the allegedly shy Shadow People. Traditional stories tell of Inuit who have crossed into the other world. No one has ever returned. No solid research yet exists in the annals of parapsychological investigation to confirm or deny this type of report.

"This actually doesn't sound so bad," Anna said, more to herself than to Sully. She didn't think he'd bother listening. "Did you read my Shadow People assignment, Sully? My research could be ground-breaking."

"If your investigation yields any results," he muttered. "And that's a big if."

Staff investigation will involve travel through Nunavut, Yukon, and the Northwest Territories. The Institute will cover staff expenses, and all travel arrangements will be coordinated through our office. Staff will be expected to interview elders to build a thorough knowledge of Inuit mythological systems. It is also the responsibility of Staff to seek out a translator/guide for fieldwork in the North.

Anna read the briefing three times before turning to Sully. "I can't believe Geoff assigned this to me."

Sully released a Mephistophelean cackle. "Have fun freezing your ass off in the Yukon."

"I will, thank you. Why? What exciting adventure did Geoff saddle to your rump?"

Sneering, Sully slid his chair back. The antiquated wheels screeched like an ambulance siren. "I need to take a piss," he announced and strode from their little workspace with his head high in the air.

"Thanks for sharing," Anna groaned, flipping through the staff assignments. And there it was: Herbert Sullivan. Even in his absence, she let out a cruel burst of laughter. This was too good. In fact, it was so good she couldn't stop herself from prancing down the hall, all the way to the men's bathroom.

Throwing open the door, she said, "Geoff stuck you in the archives, loser!"

But the delight of humiliating a peer was no sooner overshadowed by the mortification of walking in on the wrong person. Sully was nowhere to be found. The only person at the urinals was their fearless leader, Gentle Geoff.

"Anna. Oh, good. I was just coming to see you." His tone was as casual as if she'd walked in on him clearing out the break room fridge. He didn't even seem concerned when her gaze drizzled down his body and locked on one particularly delicate area.

"I..." She searched for an excuse to be standing in the men's room. "The women's doesn't work."

"Doesn't it?"

"Toilet's broken."

"Well, I'd better fix it," he replied, zipping up.

"Well, sometimes it's broken... and other times it... isn't?"

"No harm taking a quick look," he said with a shrug.

Geoff turned on the tap. As liquid soap frothed between his fingers, Anna's knees nearly gave out. She had to grasp the side of the sink just to steady herself. Suddenly he was so nearby his natural musk made her dizzy. He looked up from that hunched-over position. His face was at the same height as hers, and so close she could kiss him.

When he'd finished fixing his hair in the rust-spotted mirror, he met her gaze straight on. "I'm sorry. Were you going to...?"

With his eyes, he made a motion she couldn't comprehend. He raised his brows and shifted his gaze. What did that mean? Where was the Geoff-to-Anna translator when she needed it? Did it mean... did he want her to kiss him? Their faces were so close...

"Did you need to use the toilet?" Geoff asked, straightening up.

"What? Why?"

Plucking a paper towel from the dispenser, Geoff said, "I thought the women's was plugged. Isn't that why you're in here? To use ours?"

"Oh. Right."

"I'll just get out of your hair, then." He used his paper towel to open the grimy bathroom door.

No way was she using the disgusting boy toilet. How did she always manage to get herself into these situations? Of course it was her own fault, being so impulsive. A little self-control would go a long way, but it was so much easier to blame Sully.

"Hey jackass," she called out as she strutted back into their shared workspace. "I thought you said you were taking a piss."

"It was a metaphorical piss," Sully proclaimed with a philosophical beard rub. Holding up his refilled coffee cup, he said, "It was more like a prelude to a piss."

"Yeah, well I walked in on our boss in the crapper because of your poetic license."

"So I heard." He pointed his coffee cup in the direction of Geoff's firm ass.

"Shit," Anna exhaled. "Geoff, why are you hiding in the corner? And why are you on your hands and knees?"

"Not hiding at all," he replied, rising to his feet. "Your baseboard's coming apart. We must have mice. I'll get right on that."

"I've never had a boss who could run an entire investigative organization *and* find time for general maintenance." Sully beamed in an obvious attempt to get out of archive duty.

"Thank you," Geoff replied with a gracious grin. "That means a lot to me."

Anna leaned against their desk, wondering how she might interrupt this love fest. Now she really did have to pee. "You said you needed to talk to me?"

"That's right. I assigned you to investigate the Inuit Shadow People..."

"I know," Anna interrupted. "Thank you so much. I should have said thank you before. Thanks."

Geoff launched Sully a puzzled glance. "I'm wondering if I made the best choice. It isn't that I don't trust you to conduct a superior investigation, only that you've never done any fieldwork with the Institute."

"That's not a problem. I did fieldwork in university. I can handle it."

"I know you can, but I would feel better about sending you into the Arctic with a partner-investigator." Geoff's gaze darted toward Sully.

Double shit.

"I'll find a guide—someone who knows the North. It'll be fine. I don't need Sully to watch over me."

"Oh, I hadn't considered that option." Straightening up, Geoff tapped his fingers against the dusty bookshelf. "No, I still think I would prefer to go with you. And it has nothing to do with protection, if that's your concern. Only guidance. Applying the Institute's quality standard and all that. You know your stuff, but..."

"No, no, no, that's completely okay." Anna suppressed the urge to tackle her boss with a bear hug. "I totally get it. You're right: it's my first time out and I could definitely use your help."

"But... but... but..." Sully cut in. "You're scheduled for the Greece investigation with Sigrid. You'd rather spend your summer in the Yukon?"

With a shrug, Geoff said, "Greece has been done to death, and Sigrid's fine on her own. I've never been up North."

BY THE TIME THEY GOT around to packing their gear, every move Geoff made had Anna wondering about his intentions. What was the real reason he'd decided to come on assignment with her? He must have had ulterior motives. Sure, he didn't tease her or flirt with her or touch her casually in passing, but he wasn't generally affectionate. More one of those lost-in-thought academics.

Honestly, she wasn't sure she could handle the legwork on her own. There was a lot of research to do in very little time, and how would she have tracked down an Inuktitut translator for remote northern communities without Geoff's contacts?

They'd decided to conduct the investigation like a basic ghost hunt, which meant bringing along all the tracking equipment: video, still and infrared cameras, digital recorders, Geiger counter, parabolic microphone and of course the essential EMF detector.

The Yukon in July wasn't half as cold as she'd anticipated. Their translator, Tukkuttok, laughed as she and Geoff unpacked parkas.

"Did they mix up their seasons, do you think?" he joked with the elders. When he translated, Geoff and Anna laughed too.

Despite their mirth, though, the elders communicated very little helpful information regarding Shadow People. It's not that they had nothing to say—boy, could they talk up a storm!—only what they were saying had little bearing on the investigation.

"It is a shame when children today are not given traditional names," one elder in the Northwest Territories explained.

His wife heartily agreed, "Our young people would grow up knowing who they were if they went by traditional names. For Inuit people, our names have great meaning."

"Take Tukkuttok, for instance," Tukkuttok translated, blushing as the elder man spoke. "His name means, 'a person who is generous,' and you see how generous he is with his time?"

"Who gave you their *atiq*?" the elder asked their translator.

"*Atiq*?" Anna interrupted, flipping through her notebook. "What does that mean?"

"*Atiq* is the soul-name," Tukkuttok explained. "Names are passed from generation to generation to ensure we live on through time. I received the name of my grandmother. That means I *am* my grandmother. The connection is soul-deep, bone-to-bone. When I was a child, I replicated her behaviours and her personality traits."

"And it's okay for a boy to take after his grandmother?" Anna asked.

"Namesake is stronger than gender. Even now, I am more like my grandmother than anyone else in the world."

"Wow," Anna replied, scribbling notes in her book. "That's so..."

"Interesting," Geoff intruded, his voice brimming with impatience. After achieving no results in the Yukon, he wasn't about to meet failure in the Northwest Territories. "But what we're here to learn about is the *Tarriaksuit*. Do you know where we might begin to look for them?"

When the elders exchanged glances, Anna was certain they'd bring the interview to a close. Here these nice people were helping their investigation, offering them tea and traditional fare out of the kindness of their hearts, and Geoff was treating them like an inconvenience. She couldn't restrain herself from scolding him. "Geoff, behave."

The elders laughed, exchanging words.

"What did I miss?" Anna asked Tukkuttok. Were they laughing at her?

"They've devised Inuit names for you both," Tukkuttok said. "They call you *Illivat*, which means 'a young person who is learning.'"

"That's so nice." Anna addressed the elders. "Thank you."

"You," Tukkuttok continued, turning to Geoff, "they call *Desna*, 'the boss.'"

"Oh, that's a relief," Geoff exhaled. "I've been called far worse."

Silence cloaked the room. Anna stared down at her notebook, wishing she could scurry beneath the floorboards. Finally, the woman spoke. "Very little is known of the Shadow People."

"That's all right," Geoff said. "Just tell us what little you know. Every new piece of information helps our investigation. Where can we look for the Tarriaksuit?"

The woman looked up at her husband, as if to ask some indecipherable question. His response was, "If they want to be seen, the Shadow People will come to you."

"But do you know of any place we could go where they're more likely to appear?"

"Tarriaksuit are not the Loch Ness Monster. They do not inhabit specific spaces in our world. They live in their own world—the shadow world."

As soon as the words left the elder's lips, his wife cast him an icy glare. "We know very little of the Shadow People. I apologize if this has been a wasted journey for you."

That brought the conversation to a pretty quick close.

Trailing behind Tukkuttok on the trek back, Geoff leaned in so close Anna could feel his breath on her ear. "It seems we're being stonewalled."

"Right," Anna chuckled. "It's a conspiracy of elders across three Arctic territories."

"Keep your voice down." Geoff grabbed her forearm as he gazed up ahead at their translator.

"What, you think Tukkuttok is altering the elders' statements?" she whispered. "That doesn't make sense. You were there. You saw their reactions."

"Think about it: who set up all our meetings?"

"Tukkuttok," Anna said.

At the mention of his name, their translator turned around. "Hey slowpokes, catch up will you?"

She and Geoff must have looked like a couple of guilty rabbits, their ears perked for predators.

"Oh, I see," their guide said with a smirk. "You lovebirds want to be alone."

While Geoff offered an insincere grin, Anna felt her face flush. She concealed her obvious blush by taking off her hoodie. "Warm out today, isn't it?" She chuckled as Tukkuttok turned and went on down the path. "So you think he's been setting us up with elders he knows won't disclose anything?"

"Or maybe he warned them against sharing information on the Shadow People."

Anna raised a brow. "I think all these Arctic summer nights are making you crazy."

"Don't you worry about me. Why? Is the endless sunlight keeping you up?"

"Yeah." Anna shrugged.

"Just close the blackout blinds."

"I would, but it's fascinating... and the sun isn't *that* bright by midnight or so. Plus I'm always monitoring the equipment. Anyway, *I'm* not the conspiracy theorist here."

Geoff didn't seem to appreciate the tag, but said, "I don't know exactly what's up, but I might just get out my contact book."

In Nunuvat, Geoff found elders of his own. Or, one elder. Rather than run the risk of pissing off their translator, they visited with Tukkuttok's elders prior to stealing away to see Sakari. Her name meant *sweet*, she told them. By her welcoming manner, they were convinced they'd get some useful information from the trilingual elder.

"In addition to my mother tongue, I speak English and French. That's how I've become so well-known in my life's work."

"Sakari is a professional storyteller," Geoff told Anna, as if he hadn't already informed her when he set the appointment and again on the way over. "As you know, we're investigating the Tarriaksuit. What can you tell us about the Shadow People?"

Sakari raised her face to the sky and leaned back in her folding lawn chair. The world of the North was so quiet Anna felt unnerved by her surroundings. It was a relief when Sakari asked, "Have you ever heard the story of how Crow brought the daylight?"

"I think I read that in High School," Anna said. "No, wait, that was *Raven Steals the Light*."

"Brings, steals—it's all a matter of perspective," Sakari replied. "A very long time ago, when the world was still new, the Inuit people lived all in darkness. They had never heard of this thing called daylight, until Crow came along and explained it to them."

"Yes, this does sound familiar."

"At first, nobody believed Crow. The elders knew him to be a trickster, but the younger people were fascinated by his stories. 'If we had daylight here, we could wander far from home to hunt. We could see the polar bear before it attacks.' The young people begged Crow to bring daylight to the North. Crow agreed and started off on the long, dark journey south. When he began to see a glimmer on the horizon, he knew he was heading in the right direction."

Geoff yawned in an exaggerated manner, and Sakari gazed directly at him, saying nothing.

"Sorry," he told her. "Go on."

She waited for a moment, like she was expecting him to yawn again. When he didn't, she raised her arms in the air. "Suddenly, daylight burst upon him with its endless shades and shapes. As he perched on a tree branch, he imagined how happy the young people of the North would be when they caught their first sight of a clear blue sky and fluffy white clouds. Crow then looked down to see a beautiful woman fetching water from the river. The trickster turned himself into a seed and drifted down to settle into the woman's cloak. When she returned home, he found how lucky he was. This girl was the daughter of the village chief."

"What village?" Anna asked, but Geoff set a hand on her knee as if to stifle her. His touch sent a giddy blaze through her body, and she hugged her notebook tight to her chest.

The storyteller ignored her question, at any rate, and went on with the legend. "Inside the chief's lodge, Crow spotted a box that glowed around the edges. Daylight! On the floor, the woman's little son played with the prized box. In the form of a seed, Crow drifted into the little boy's ear. The child cried and cried, but his mother couldn't comfort him. The boy called out for his kindly grandfather.

"'Why are you crying?' the chief asked the little one.

"From within the boy's ear, Crow whispered: 'I want to play with the ball of daylight.' The child rubbed his ear and repeated Crow's words.

"The chief removed the ball of light from its casing without a second thought. But again the boy cried and when the chief asked why, he spoke Crow's words: 'I want to play outside.' And so the chief lifted up the small child and carried him to the river.

"As soon as they reached the clearing, Crow swooped out of the child's ear and regained his true form. He grabbed the ball of light and flew across the sky, trailing daylight behind him.

"Through the darkness, the Northern people saw a spark of light coming toward them. It grew brighter and brighter, until Crow dropped the ball. It shattered on the ground and daylight exploded, illuminating every dark place and chasing away every shadow. The sky became bright and blue. Dark mountains took on colour and form. Snow and ice sparkled so brightly our people had to shade their eyes.

"But Crow warned them daylight would not last forever. He only brought one ball of daylight, and it would need to rest for six months every year to regain its strength. During that six-month period, the darkness would return. To this day, the people of the North live for half a year in darkness and half a year in daylight. They are always kind to Crow, for it was he who brought the light."

As Anna scribbled madly in her notebook, Geoff let out a huff. "Do you have any stories about the Shadow People?"

Sakari pulled her shawl around her shoulders. "The chill is setting in early tonight." Rising from her lawn chair, she said, "I think I'll be heading in now. Very nice to make your acquaintance. Safe journey to you both."

Geoff shot out of his seat, knocking it over in the process, then kicked the storyteller's abandoned chair. "Well that just tears it!"

Anna thanked her lucky stars Sakari had gone inside, but she felt positively stupefied by his behaviour. "What the hell, Geoff? What is wrong with you?"

"I could have spent the summer in Greece."

"You said..."

"And instead I'm stuck here in the land of the midnight *sun* on a failed investigation with little miss *sunshine* herself."

His words hit Anna's chest like a brick, but she didn't want him to see how badly he'd hurt her. Painting on a smile, she tried to brighten his mood. "We won't have failed until we've totally given up."

"No wonder we can't track Shadow People." Geoff stomped over to their borrowed truck. "Your *sunny disposition* is driving them all away!"

Anna didn't know what to say. Nobody had ever characterised her as an optimist before. Why did it feel like such an insult?

She tried not to look at her boss on the drive back. His squirrelly face sparked a rage made more intense by the memory of attraction.

"I don't understand why you're being like this," she said, staring straight ahead.

"Like what?" he challenged, his tone icy cold.

"You know what I used to call you? Gentle Geoff. That was you: always kind to everybody, whether they'd been at the Institute for a thousand years or they were just interning for a couple months. You always showed everyone respect, so why are you treating me like shit?"

"Get a grip." He didn't take his eyes off the road. "Look, tonight I'm taking the tracking equipment up to that lake by the old lady's lodge. She's hiding something—I can feel it."

Three months ago, the idea of another all-nighter with Geoff would have set her heart palpitating. Now she wished she could call in sick. "Fine. Can we at least grab a bite first? I'm starving."

"You're not coming with me. Stay at the lodge and pull those blackout blinds. You need your sleep."

Rage boiled beneath Anna's skin, making her brusque. Channelling her teenaged self, she growled, "Whatever," and left it at that.

THE LODGE MADE A DELICIOUS moose meat burger, and Anna gave in to it, and fries and a bottle of red, in her room. She couldn't stand the idea of interacting with people.

Leaving her destroyed plate of dinner outside the door, she switched off the lamp and joined her wine glass on the reading chair by the window. The view was truly extraordinary.

The evening sun shone like a comet in the sky, resisting the pressure of dusk as Anna resisted the call of sleep. Her eyelids tumbled, bouncing apart each time they met, until finally they closed and rested together. She envisioned Crow coursing through the darkness, trailing daylight behind him like a banner for new beginnings. She saw the young people cheering him on and their parents clucking about the old ways. Fearful of the radiance Crow brought, they hid in the...

"My God," Anna cried, bolting upright in her chair. "We've been so stupid! The elders have been answering our questions all along—we just weren't listening."

As soon as the words crossed her lips, the blackout blinds on her window snapped shut and the barely-visible nightlight in the bathroom flickered off. Sheer blackness enveloped the room, and she knew the answer even before she asked, "Who's there?"

Her voice sounded small in the darkness. It echoed all alone in a cavernous realm. A bottomless sense of grief overtook her and she wept uncontrollably into her wine glass. It was the only thing still connecting her to the material world, and she grasped its stem with all her strength.

There was so much pain in life. Just look at Geoff: she put her hopes in him and he treated her like crap. That's what happens when we have hopes: they're inevitably stomped on by so-called benevolent forces.

The blinds sprung open and a dazzling light caressed Anna from outside. In fact, for a moment, there was only light and nothing else. It filled her heart with such warmth she was sure her chest would explode.

This must be death. What else could it be?

And then the light subsided. She now realized she was outside the lodge. She looked in the window to see herself passed out in the reading chair, still grasping her wine glass. In the window's reflection, she watched as rays of light flickered from the sky and manifested a form. The form was a man, and the man was spectacular.

She had every reason to be afraid, but she wasn't. Her heart and mind were utterly at ease as she watched him approach her like a spectre in the window's reflection. His round face would have been haunting were it not for the smile on his lips. In the window's reflection, the contrast between his skin and his black hair appeared stark, but when she turned to look at him straight on it seemed less obvious.

"Oh my god!" Erupting with laughter, Anna covered her mouth. "I'm sorry! I have no idea who you are and I know I shouldn't say this, but what the hell are you wearing?"

His pants, cut just below the knee, seemed to be some kind of eccentric twist on traditional Inuit dress.

Placing his hands on his hips, the hot phantom snapped, "Shut your mouth, girl. Have you ever hand-sewn rhinestones into caribou skin?"

"Can't say as I have," she snickered.

"I figured. Took me half a year to make these dance pants."

"Okay, dude..."

Sucking his teeth, he said, "My pants kick your dress' ass."

"Dress?" Anna glanced down. Where were her flannel pyjamas? Why was she wearing this shapeless hide shift? "This isn't mine. I don't know..."

The man whipped around to strut down the lake path. "Follow me, girlfriend."

"Oh, so we're friends now, are we?"

"Yes, Illivat."

Her heart leapt with inexplicable affinity for the ghost. Her pulse quickened. This all felt unreal, like she was floating above the situation and participating at the same time.

"We're going to be good friends soon, you and me and Kattituyok."

"If you say so." She grinned, hopping to keep up. "Who is Katti...?"

"Kattituyok: he who has a deep voice."

"Who are you?" Anna asked as they headed toward a lake that sparkled in the late-night sun.

"Pikatti," he said simply.

She felt like one of those kids who would keep asking questions until you shoved a lollipop in her mouth. "Are you Tarriaksuit, you and Katti...?" She mumbled the end of his name because she couldn't remember it.

Pikatti turned to face her with the lake glistening behind him. "Kattituyok."

That obviously didn't answer her question.

"What is Tarriaksuit?" asked a booming voice over Anna's shoulder.

She spun on her heels to see who was there.

A man slightly older than Pikatti stood before her. He wore caribou pants with a fringe, but sadly lacking rhinestones. His presence made Anna uneasy, but not because she was afraid; he just seemed so illustrious she felt she didn't deserve to occupy the same space as him. His greatness drove her to Pikatti's side. An Inuit ghost wearing rhinestones seemed pretty safe, in comparison.

"Shadow People," Anna replied in a voice smaller than her own. "I'm a parapsychologist... kind of... well, I will be once I've chosen a thesis topic. Anyway, you don't care about that. Basically, I'm in the North looking for Tarriaksuit."

The man with the big strong chest smirked like he had a secret. "You're not alone."

Just to their right, he indicated the Institute's camera equipment perched on a boulder. Behind it, a man sat very still, his eyes glued to an EMF reader.

She smiled so hard her jaw hurt. "Oh my god! Geoff!"

He didn't react. He didn't seem to hear her, or even pick up her body heat on the thermo-cam.

"Looking for Tarriaksuit?" Pikatti taunted. "Girl, you *are* Tarriaksuit. And that guy can't see you any more than he can see me or Kattituyok."

Shadow People! She almost couldn't believe it, even though she knew it was true. After all the cloak and dagger from the elders, she'd found them. Anna felt like royalty. She was in the Shadow World.

With a child's buoyancy, she looked Pikatti up and down and chuckled. "The stories say you're shy."

"Yes, terribly," Pikatti sighed, throwing a melodramatic arm around her shoulder.

Kattituyok huffed. "Anyone who steps into this world of ours realizes at once they wouldn't dream of leaving."

"Your world accepts voyagers from ours, then?" Anna asked, wishing she had her notebook.

"From yours or any other. We wish to preserve the integrity of our world, but not to the exclusion of any interested party."

"I'm interested," Anna said, auspiciously.

"We know, Illivat. That is why we've appeared to you."

"But Goeff..." She glanced in his direction. He was looking straight through her. "He's interested too. Why can't you bring him here?"

"Your colleague comes to judge us."

"No, Geoff wants to understand you. He's a knowledge-seeker."

"But he would reveal us to your world," Pikatti interjected.

"So would I. That's what I came up here to do: find you guys and write a report on you. Why won't you let Geoff into your world? He wants to find it so badly. He'll go home in shreds if I get to meet you and he doesn't."

"I can't comprehend why you would care so much about a man who denigrates you," Kattituyok said, shaking his head.

"He doesn't," she argued, reflecting, and not quite believing herself. "I think he's just stressed. He doesn't deal well with failure."

"Somebody's making excuses," Pikatti replied, tickling her sides. As she gave in and giggled, he whispered, "Our little Illivat deserves better."

Anna stopped laughing and looked up almost in despair at the solemn but kind warrior before her. "Kattituyok...please tell me who you are. We've asked so many elders and they had nothing to say."

"Of course not," Kattituyok replied. "Our world is quite insular."

"It's not as dark as I pictured it," she admitted, gazing up at the sun. It wasn't quite beaming—not this late at night—more like hovering in space. "Why is it called the shadow world?"

"You think this is the shadow world? No, no, no." Pikatti chuckled. "That's our name for where you live. If you saw your world from where we stand, you'd think you were living in the shadows too."

An idea dawned on her like a two-by-four to the back of the head. *I've been living in the shadow all this time.* Dizzied, she swerved until she was somehow on her knees. Even her head was too heavy to support, and she let it fall to the gravel beach. The ground was cold, but her body was steaming-hot as she rested in the giddy bliss of a drunken stupor.

"Why do I feel like this?" she asked, feeling flighty and faint.

"You are coming to an important realization," Kattituyok replied.

She nodded against the damp, gritty sand. "Geoff doesn't like me."

Pikatti knelt beside her, petting her back. "That's not the important bit. What else have you got?"

Squeezing her eyes shut, she fought back tears. "He's treating me like shit and I deserve so, so, so much better."

"Yes, Illivat," the sage one said. "And?"

"I'm always getting in my own way. I get attached to these jerks, and then when I realize how bad they are for me I can't get rid of him. Like stupid Sully—I was crazy for him in University. Even now that I see how bad he is for me, I'm still

105

sharing an office with the bastard. I can't get these assholes out of my life!"

Pikatti rubbed her back until her soft dress fell forward, fell down her back and covered her head. She pulled out of it, sitting it under her head to keep her face off the beach. Pikatti's warm touch felt so much better against her bare flesh. His hand felt like seal pelt as it brushed her ass, which she held high in the air. It moved down her thighs to tickle her feet.

"Do you get it now?" Pikatti asked.

Kittituyok didn't give her an opportunity to answer. "Anna is the shadow. Illivat walks in the sun."

"Illivat," she repeated. "We were the Shadow People. Goeff and I couldn't find the shadow world because we were already in it."

"Now we start you on your new path." Pikatti traced his fingers across her inner thigh. "In our world, only fear is condemned. Whatever is not love is fear."

Anna caught him looking at Kattituyok with a combination of desire and reverence. The sage responded with a deep-voiced chuckle and a smirk. Pikatti's smile grew wider as his fingers peeked inside the waist of Kattituyok's fringed caribou pants.

Kattituyok declared, "In your world, people see only difference."

"With us, anything goes." Pikatti pulled down the caribou hide.

Kattituyok gasped at the younger man's touch and then said to Anna, "You revile each other for your diversity."

Pikatti grasped Kattituyok's cock and pumped it slowly. He slipped his soft-as-pelt hand between Anna's thighs. When he squeezed mound, she exploded like a juiced orange, melting into the beach. What could she do but surrender to their wisdom and their world? She was theirs now. She belonged to this place.

"In this world, we are as one," Pikatti continued, stroking her wet pussy. She rocked for him, moving back and forth to increase the sensation of his touch against her throbbing clit. The more she moaned, the more Kattituyok moaned, and his derivative pleasure increased her own. Pikatti pleased them both.

"Here, there is reciprocity to desire." Kattituyok hissed as Pikatti grasped his balls in a firm grip. "We fulfil each other's wants and needs."

"Whatever you want to give, you can always find someone to take it," Pikatti continued.

"And anything you wish to receive can be granted by a willing partner."

"Like right now I want to give Kattituyok head..." Pikatti said.

"...and I wish to receive it," Kattituyok replied, his voice smooth and deep as chocolate.

Leaning to her ear, Pikatti whispered, "What about you, Illivat? What do you want to give? What do you wish to receive?"

Those two simple questions brought tears to her eyes. Not once in her life had anyone asked what she wanted of a sexual encounter. She mumbled a response neither could make out.

"Louder, Illivat," Pikatti encouraged. "Tell us what you want."

She summoned her core strength and released her response. "I want to give and take. I want to give you my pussy. I want to take your cock inside me."

"Ahhh," Kattituyok purred.

Like gears in motion, the men clicked into place. Gravel shifted underfoot as Pikatti slipped out of his quirky caribou pants. Kattituyok stood strong above her, straddling her waiting body. Even naked with her face to foreign soil and her rump high in the air, Anna was invulnerable. After all, this was a different world.

With Kattituyok's firm calf blocking the way, she could just make out Pikatti's glistening form coming at her. He gripped the base of his cock, asking, "Is this what you want?"

Her heart pounded. "Yes," she replied, bracing for entry.

Gripping her hips, he chuckled, "Well, then, I won't deny you your pleasure."

In one majestic motion, he slid inside her body and made it his home. He was huge inside her, but she made room because, god, did she ever want him there. That space had been reserved for a cock like his. She just didn't know it until now.

"And I will not deny you your pleasure," Kattituyok boomed. No sooner had he spoken than a muffled exultation erupted from Pikatti's throat.

Try as she might, Anna couldn't turn far enough to catch a glimpse of Kattituyok's impressive cock filling his fit young lover's mouth. She'd love to watch. Was Pikatti sucking the hell out of that beast, or simply sitting back and taking it as the gorgeous sage fucked his welcoming throat? She couldn't quite tell what was going on above her.

An icy thought struck her as she looked to the right. "Are you sure Geoff can't see us?"

Kattituyok chuckled deeply as Pikatti replied, "If he could see all this, do you really think he'd have his nose in a book?"

"You're right," Anna said, relaxing as Pikatti ran his sharp nails along her back. The sensation of delicious pain made her moan. Her pussy devoured his cock as he devoured Kattituyok's. It struck her how pussy-like a mouth is: wet, warm, welcoming, and satiny-soft. Mouths and pussies were nearly the same thing.

With Pikatti gripping her thighs, she reached up to feel her engorged clit. Her own wetness heightened her arousal, and she stroked herself into a frenzy as he fucked her needy cunt. She let that big cock slide between her two fingers and felt a sense of accomplishment when Pikatti gasped in response.

"Oh god," she panted in time with the men's crescendo of grunts and moans. There was nothing hotter than Pikatti's gurgle of approval as he thrust in her cunt and Kattiutuyok thrust in his mouth.

Turning from the vision of Geoff a world away, she grasped Kattituyok's ankle, which was firm like a teenaged tree. She was nearing the brink and needed more than Pikatti alone could give. Revelling in the deep moans of their male sex, she rubbed her clit mercilessly, fingers dancing with Pikatti's rapidly-thrusting cock. She reached far back to grab his balls and everything happened all at once. Suddenly, their collective pleasure overwhelmed them.

Kattituyok bellowed high above her, his cry and his cock stifling Pikatti's orgasmic groan. She didn't need to hear it to know. His hands kneaded her ass cheeks, grasped them hard as he rammed her one last time. Dizzied by pleasure beyond anything she'd ever imagined, she let her hand fall to earth when Pikatti held still, his massive cock pulsing inside her. She could feel herself trembling, but his cock was hers for a few more moments.

Impressively, Kattituyok remained standing even as she and Pikatti collapsed. She couldn't wipe the smile off her face, even after lying naked on the beach under the midnight sun. She was safe, she knew, with a strong man standing guard.

"This is nuts." She laughed, catching sight of Pikatti's rhinestone caribou pants. "Is this for real? Have I seriously left the world I came from?"

Nobody answered. They didn't need to; she knew where she was.

Behind the big boulder, Geoff had fallen asleep. She'd never seen him sleep before. He looked like an old man. And he snored.

"I've tried all my life to be accepted by... well, anybody, really. You guys brought me here and took me in, welcomed me, initiated me into your world..."

She wondered what Geoff might find when he reviewed the images his video recorder had picked up. More than likely, he'd go home knowing next to nothing about the Shadow People. He'd go home feeling like a failure. And he'd go home never knowing where Anna had disappeared to.

Traditional stories tell of Inuit who have crossed into the other world. No one has ever returned...

© 2008 Giselle Renarde

Anal Angel

Clarice bundled the package under her coat to sneak it past her roommates.

It's not that she was particularly embarrassed about her affliction—okay, maybe she was *a little* embarrassed—but if she told Jason and Tariq she experienced chronic anal fissures they'd insist she see a doctor. When you tell people your ass is bleeding, they tend to overreact.

It's not that Clarice disliked doctors as people, more that the whole medical establishment pissed her off. They'd send her for test after test and ultimately decide she just needed to live with the problem. By dealing with the issue on her own, she'd save herself the ordeal of having strangers poke and prod at her ass.

That's why she'd ordered Anal Angel online: an herbal product, a little on the pricey side and there was no guarantee it would work, but Clarice was getting desperate. Her fissures were coming more frequently, and every time a new one sliced its way across her anus she felt like she was being knifed in the butt.

Not pleasant.

When she got to her room, Clarice opened the bubble enveloped she'd just picked up at the post office. She slid its contents onto the bed: one small tincture bottle made of dark glass, with a squeezy dropper thing at the top. She opened the lid and took a sniff. The soothing scent of chamomile filled her bedroom.

Just as her body started to relax there was a knock at her door.

"Don't come in! Don't come in!" She crammed the lid back on the tincture, trying to fit it on without spilling any liquid.

"Why?" Tariq said from the other side. "Are you flicking your bean in there?"

Jason laughed along. "We're gonna hit The Head, then maybe a late show. Wanna come with?"

"No thanks," Clarice said.

"Just one drink?" Tariq asked.

"Not tonight, guys."

Jason jiggled the handle to tease her. "You used to be cool."

When she'd first moved in with them, Jason did that a lot: jiggle the door handle in the middle of the night and pretend the house was haunted. It freaked her out, but every time she told the guys about it, they'd crack up. Eventually she realized it was just a trick to scare her.

"Your loss," the guys said.

Clarice slid the tincture and its envelope under her pillow, and then stepped out of her room. She followed the guys and said, "Next Friday, okay? I'm just feeling kinda icky tonight."

They looked up at her from the bottom of the stairs, and their expressions shifted from amusement to concern. Tariq asked, "You want us to stay home?"

"No, no. You guys go."

Jason cocked his head. "You're sure?"

"Yeah, it's no big deal. I'll feel better in the morning."

They seemed satisfied, and Clarice was glad to see them go. She loved the guys, but the online reviews for her tincture claimed it was "magic" and she wanted the place to herself while it worked.

Clarice ran herself a bath and luxuriated much longer than she would have if the guys had been home. Afterwards, when her skin felt clean and glowing, she perched over the toilet and opened her tincture. That subtle chamomile scent infused the steamy bathroom, and her muscles fell even more deeply into relaxation mode.

She'd read the instructions online before she'd bought it. Simple enough: squeeze one drop onto a clean finger and press against the fissure. She held her breath as she brought the pad of her middle finger to her ass, following the pain.

"Magic" was, perhaps, an oversell.

The tincture warmed her ass, especially where the skin was split. Perhaps its healing properties would kick into gear after a few days of use, but from the reviews she'd read online Clarice really thought the fissure would heal itself the moment that soft liquid touched her skin.

With a sigh, Clarice screwed the cap back on and hid the tincture in a box of tampons—somewhere the guys would never look. She hung up her towel and tossed a robe around her shoulders, then stepped out of the bathroom.

The hallway was dark, but a warm light glowed from inside her bedroom. What was that? She hadn't left her lamp on.

A cold sweat broke at the small of her back. Her muscles clenched.

"Hello?" Clarice called out. "Is someone there?"

The light grew brighter as a body stepped into the frame of her open door. Who was that? A woman. Someone she didn't know. Someone with hair that was snow-white, but skin that wasn't.

The woman's nearly-naked form glowed a light shade of purple or blue—Clarice couldn't tell which. She wore only two scraps of clothing: denim cut-offs and a tank top with the words Anal Angel splashed across the front. No bra. Her erect nipples shone a darker shade of purply-blue right through the fabric.

"Don't be afraid, Clarice."

"I... I... I'm not afraid."

Yeah-fucking-right she wasn't. She probably would have shit herself if shitting didn't hurt so damn badly.

"You've purchased my service," the woman said. "I'm your anal angel."

Clarice shook her head—or, her head shook itself. She didn't feel like she was totally in control of anything right now. "Service? I bought... a product, a tincture. It's in the bathroom."

"Anal Angel is more than just a bottle."

"Let me guess," Clarice said. "It's a genie, too?"

The woman's gentle smile lit up the hallway. "Close. You've very close."

When the woman retreated to the bedroom, Clarice followed her. "How did you get in my house? What are you doing in my bedroom? Who are you, some kind of metaphysical customer service rep?"

Her eyes brightened. "An angelic customer service rep, I suppose you'd say."

Clarice stood in the doorway while the buxom blonde stretched out on her bed. "You're an angel? For real? Like, a real live angel sent from heaven to take care of my ass?"

"You paid for the service. I'm your anal angel." She pointed to the door and it magically shut, sweeping Clarice inside. "Let's start the healing process, shall we? You've endured too many years of pain."

Tightening her robe, Clarice said, "I didn't want to see a doctor."

"A doctor couldn't help you, love. What you need is cosmic intervention. Undress for me, and lie face-down on the bed."

Clarice shrugged off her robe, letting it pool at her feet. "This is kind of insane. You know that, right? If it wasn't for your weird glowing skin I'd be calling the police right now."

The angel smirked, exploring Clarice's fresh nudity with her eyes. "It's been so long for you, hasn't it?"

Clarice's nipples hardened against the cool night air. "What, with the fissures? Yeah, it's been chronic."

Angel laughed. "That's not what I meant."

Her soft gaze hardened into a steely fire, and Clarice felt suddenly taken aback. This wasn't some holistic angel-doctor's examination table. That scintillating woman wanted to give her more than just a healing touch.

"What are you doing?" Clarice asked. Suddenly, her lower half started to tingle all the way from her ass to her clit. It wasn't the usual fiery roar of arousal, though. This tingle felt cool, strange. Like she'd slathered Vicks all over her pussy and down her crack.

"Come," Angel said. "Trust me. It's all part of the service."

"I do trust you," Clarice said, despite herself.

This night was getting just plain weird.

Angel extended her hand and Clarice grasped it, allowing the stranger to pull her toward the bed.

She didn't even feel her feet moving. It was like standing on a raft, being drawn slowly across a river. She climbed up on her mattress, completely naked, and kneeled next to the magical woman. Angel stared at her bare breasts unapologetically, and Clarice cupped them—not so much out of shame, but more to lift them up and make them look a bit better.

"What now?" she asked.

Angel tilted her head, letting her hair cascade over one purply-blue shoulder. "I have a task at hand, but I'm willing to veer off course in any direction you'd like. Tell me how long it's been."

Something gnawed at Clarice's gut. At first she thought the question had angered her, but she soon realized she was upset by the answer. "Zafira broke up with me almost a year ago. I haven't been able to... I haven't *wanted* to... with anyone else, you know? I haven't even looked at another woman, not in a serious way."

"You loved her so hard." Angel's hand rode Clarice's thigh, gently at first. Then she squeezed, showing she understood, she'd been there too. "Zafira stole your heart and you're afraid you'll never find it again. You don't know where she put it."

Clarice's whole body tensed, from her shoulders to her asshole. "I don't want to talk about this."

"You don't have to." Angel swept forward, like linens on a breeze, wrapping herself around Clarice. "Relax. Just relax. Everything's going to be just fine."

Once Angel's lips found her skin, they were everywhere at once—kissing her neck, her shoulders, her chest, her chin. One hand dove between Clarice's thighs, parting them only slightly, but enough to find the juice of her arousal and the clean, hot bud of her clit.

The stranger smelled like lilies. Overwhelmingly sweet. Clarice struggled to breathe that thick perfume while Angel touched her. That touch was magic. It made her body tingle.

"Kiss me," Clarice whispered, and in moments Angel's soft lips pressed against hers.

It didn't just stop at lips. The stranger's gentle tongue slipped against Clarice's teeth, begging entry, which Clarice wholeheartedly granted. She returned the angel's kiss with a passion she thought she'd lost when Zafira left.

She took Angel's face in her hands and kissed, kissed, kissed.

"Please," Clarice begged. She didn't even know what she was asking for, but when Angel kissed her neck, she repeated that word over and over. "Please, oh please, oh please!"

Angel's soft fingers parted her pussy lips and found her swollen clit. "Untouched for a year," Angel said. "You won't even touch yourself."

How could she possibly have known that? She must truly be a metaphysical being, to mystically know Clarice had put a moratorium on masturbation.

"Why?" Angel asked.

Tears formed in Clarice's eyes. "It always made me think of her."

Angel kissed a path down Clarice's chest and, before taking a nipple between her lips, said, "Tell me."

117

The second Angel began to suckle, a tear escaped and rolled down Clarice's cheek. It clung momentarily to her chin, then took a tumble, landing in Angel's white hair.

Sniffling back an onslaught of tears, Clarice said, "Every time I tried, I'd picture her face between my legs. I'd see her down there, licking me like she did, and it made me so sad. It made me want her back. Then I'd remember how much she hurt me, and I just... couldn't. I couldn't be happy. I can't be happy without her."

Releasing Clarice's nipple, Angel said, "Anal fissures can be cause by stress. Did they begin around the time of the breakup?"

Clarice thought back, and felt her head expanding as she nodded. "Yeah, actually—or, they definitely got worse."

"Well, then," Angel said, falling to her knees at the side of the bed. "Let's replace those painful memories with pleasurable ones."

Pressing Clarice's thighs open, Angel bowed between them. Clarice couldn't help but watch as the woman opened her mouth to expose a tongue unlike any she'd ever seen. It looked like the stranger had been sucking on Lifesavers. Her tongue was totally blue—ocean blue. The colour of healing.

Clarice's clit throbbed with that same icy-cool sensation she'd felt before.

But instead of licking, Angel pulled back. Gazing up at Clarice, she asked, "Do you want to be healed?"

"Yes," Clarice said. "Of course I do. That's why I bought Anal Angel. That's why I bought... YOU, I guess."

The stranger blushed, turning her bluish cheeks an unmistakeable shade of purple. "I will do everything I can to help you."

Angel spread Clarice's pussy lips with her thumbs, bowed gently between her thighs, and planted a long, luxurious lick all the way up to her clit.

Clarice seized when the stranger's tongue touched the bud of her arousal. Not only because it had been so long since she'd been touched there. Not only because she'd forgotten how incredible another woman's mouth could feel. But mostly because Angel's tongue didn't feel like anything she'd ever encountered.

Angel's tongue was a strange combination of cool and hot. Her saliva was like some sort of muscle rub that started out tingly and cold, then slowly an underlying warm sensation rose up, as if out of nowhere, and her entire mound felt swollen and tender—in the best way possible.

When Angel wrapped those lovely purple lips around Clarice's clit, boy was she ever glad the guys had gone out! It felt so good to let go and shriek with delight. Angel sucked her clit into that strange cool-and-hot tingly mouth, and Clarice wiggled on the bed to give the stranger better access.

Angel slipped her hands beneath Clarice's naked ass and cupped both cheeks eagerly. When the stranger propped her up a little higher off the bed, Clarice fell back. She giggled when her head landed on the bouncy mattress. It had been so long since she'd felt that kind of carefree joy. She cupped her breasts and gazed down just in time to watch Angel lifting her ass a little higher.

"What are you doing?" she asked the stranger.

Angel slowly parted Clarice's ass cheeks with the palms of her hands. "Taking care of you, Clarice."

She had a sinking feeling she knew what that meant, but she couldn't be certain... until Angel's icy-warm tongue lapped her crack.

Every muscle in Clarice's body seized. "Angel!"

Angel gazed up at her with those beautiful turquoise eyes and said, "Yes, my dear?"

She didn't know how to respond. "You can't... you can't..."

Smiling gently, the stranger assured her, "I am your Anal Angel, Clarice. The tincture was only the start. It needs to be activated by the power within me."

"Oh." Clarice considered the pain she'd experienced over the course of the past year. If Angel could cure the fissures with her tongue, Clarice had to let her or risk living the rest of her life in extreme knife-like pain. "Okay, then."

"Relax," Angel said, rising to her feet. "Close your eyes and breathe."

Clarice cheated and kept her eyes open just a slit. And she was glad she did, because she got to watch the mysterious stranger unbuttoning her shorts and slowly pulling down the zipper. Angel pushed those denim short-shorts down her thighs.

She wasn't wearing any underwear, and her pubic hair was the same colour as her head hair: brilliant, shining white. White like the sun.

Clarice throbbed as she watched the woman undress.

She already knew Angel wasn't wearing a bra, but her body went crazy as the stranger pulled that branded tank top over her head. Angel's long hair spilled over her shoulders and she tossed it around, but Clarice truly couldn't steal her gaze away from the woman's bountiful breasts. They were full and fleshy, with perky purple nipples pointing straight ahead.

As she observed the naked woman between her legs, a strange thing happened: Clarice's asshole started throbbing, same as her clit. She craved the woman's tongue not only on her pussy, but between her cheeks, too.

Clarice quit cheating and opened her eyes wide.

Angel grinned as if to say, "Naughty girl. I didn't say you could look!"

Clarice returned her smile, wondering what could possibly happen next. Angel obviously had something planned. But what?

Kneeling on either side of Clarice's thighs, Angel slowly dropped her naked body down. Angel's beautiful breasts were the first portion of her anatomy to touch Clarice's. The sensation defied belief. When Angel's pointy purple tits touched Clarice's boring beige nipples, it was like a lightning exchange between them. Clarice felt it not only in her clit, but in her asshole too.

"Oh God," she said, touching her fingers to Angel's sides. "Oh, that feels so good."

Angel lowered herself a little more, until her breasts pressed into Clarice's and their hip bones clanged together. Clarice could feel the woman's tight belly against her curved one, and then the smooth skin of their thighs touching. Finally, the whisper of Angel's glowing white pubic hair met with hers and her whole body shuddered.

Clarice let her hands wander the new terrain of Angel's ass. Oh, her skin felt so soft, so cool, so different from anything else she'd touched.

Their lips met as they writhed together on the bed. They kissed and rolled, landing with Clarice on top and then Clarice the one below. For a magical moment, they were nothing but a tangled mess of limbs and tongues.

That's when the urge overcame her, and she said to Angel, "Let me taste you. *Please*."

Without hesitation, Angel climbed Clarice's body and covered her mouth with the sweetest pussy she'd ever tasted.

Angel rocked on Clarice's mouth, doing the work for her. All Clarice had to do was languidly lick and enjoy the nectar of her angel's arousal.

But soon the taste of pussy wasn't enough. Even as she watched Angel hug those big breasts and bounce on her face, she craved something altogether different.

Clarice wanted to lick the angel's ass.

It wasn't something she'd ever considered doing with another human. But Angel was a mystical being. Did she even have an asshole? Well, if she did, it would surely be as sweet and clean as her slippery cunt.

Without notifying the stranger, Clarice started working her way down the woman's body. Angel kept adjusting her position so her perfect purple clit would strike Clarice's tongue, but when the range expired, Angel asked, "Where are you going?"

"Ummm..." Clarice couldn't answer. She was too embarrassed about what she wanted to try.

"Ohhh," Angel said, nodding as she walked her knees up the bed. "Not a word. I understand completely."

Angel set her ass over Clarice's face, and the world went darker than before. The stranger's position on the bed blocked out the lamp light, and a panic sensation seized Clarice's heart. She didn't know what she was doing. She'd never tried this before. She couldn't even see the angel's asshole.

As it turned out, she didn't need to.

Clarice pressed her palms against Angel's cheeks, spreading them wide. Her crack smelled of lilacs, which was a good start.

She stuck out her tongue and felt around. Angel's crack was almost as soft as her pussy had been, but where was her hole? Maybe she didn't have one.

"Keep going," Angel told her. "Almost there."

Clarice walked her tongue up the stranger's crack, poking tentatively until she found a spot that felt different.

"Oh!" Angel gasped.

This was it—Angel's purple pucker. Clarice had found it. But what now?

"Lick it," Angel pleaded, sounding rather desperate.

Clarice licked it, paying particular attention to the rise and fall and rise again. It was like sweeping her tongue across a very soft volcano—and one that tasted of pretty things, of flowers and springtime.

But the little lick didn't seem to do much for Angel.

Clarice made her tongue straight and hard, and pressed it forcefully into Angel's hole. That must have shocked the stranger, because her pucker opened up long enough for Clarice to stick her tongue inside.

Angel's pucker then locked down around Clarice's tongue. With anyone else, she'd have panicked. After all, her tongue was stuck within the vice grip of a stranger's asshole. But with Angel, she simply pressed those cheeks apart and worked up a bit of momentum.

She fucked the stranger's asshole with her tongue, and in time Angel got into the groove. Angel bounced a bit, lifting her body and letting it fall rather forcefully on Clarice's face. Clarice had to push up on the woman's ass to keep herself from getting crushed.

Still, she wasn't afraid. She could barely breathe and she couldn't swallow, but she wasn't scared.

After all, the stranger was an angel—*her* angel, who'd come to cure *her* affliction. Angel wouldn't let any arm come to her. So she just kept tongue-fucking the woman's glorious ass, choking on saliva, digging her fingers into that delicious blue butt and gurgling with the pleasure of doing something positively dirty.

Clarice watched as the stranger reached down and fluttered her fingers across her very purple clit. Clarice had a much better view of Angel's pussy than of her ass, so it was easy to see her labia flutter with gratitude and her slit pump out even more sparkling nectar.

There was so much pussy juice pumping from Angel's cunt that it filled Clarice's mouth. Something more to choke on while the stranger rubbed that clit and rode her tongue.

Angel's voice was like music when she came. In fact, it must have bounced weirdly off the walls, because she sounded not like one individual singing Clarice's praises, but like a whole choir. Bells were ringing somewhere in the distance. The hills rejoiced.

And Clarice's clit throbbed like a massively engorged cock.

She sputtered and coughed when Angel rolled off, panting, "Sorry, I got a bit carried away, didn't I?"

"It's okay," Clarice told her. "Don't worry about it—just do me. And fast!"

It wasn't until Angel had climbed down her body that Clarice realized her mouth was numb. That must have been an effect of the stranger's unusual bodily fluids, which obviously had healing qualities. She moved her mouth around, but it felt like she'd been sucking on an ice cube.

Good thing she wouldn't need it for now.

Angel flipped Clarice onto her front and hoisted her bum in the air. All that was left on the mattress were Clarice's boobs, head, and arms. Standing beside the bed, Angel planted her face between Clarice's butt cheeks and licked her hole like it was going out of style.

All the blood rushed to Clarice's head, making her feel like she was spinning. She got that strange dizzy sensation in her pelvis, which made her clit throb even faster. She tried to move her hand, but the dizziness made her uncoordinated. As much as she wanted to, she found she couldn't budge.

With both thighs on Angel's shoulders and her feet kicking air behind the woman's back, Clarice felt like she was swimming while the stranger sucked her asshole. The whole experience was dreamlike and weird. She didn't feel perfectly conscious, but she also didn't feel like she was dreaming. This world seemed, if anything, more *real* than the one she usually inhabited.

In this world, there were white-haired angels who could throw you over their shoulders and eat your ass until you screamed. In this world, you could let a stranger devour your hole and not even feel ashamed. If anything, you'd feel proud because she seemed to derive so much pleasure from sucking your pucker.

Clarice moaned into the rumpled bedspread. Her mouth still wouldn't make words, but at least it could make noise. She inched her hand down the bed and tried to reach her clit. Raising her arm off the mattress made her feel seasick.

"Ohhh," Clarice groaned while the stranger parted her bum cheeks and poked a superbly large tongue inside. "Ohhh... ohhh!"

Is this what it felt like to be butt-fucked? She'd never tried it before. She was too afraid it would be messy and hurt like hell, especially considering her ceaseless fissures.

But this? This felt incredible!

Angel's tongue felt thick and cylindrical inside her. It entered easily, like it was coated in some sort of magical lubricant. Her sensitive skin tingled icy-hot everywhere Angel's tongue touched. Icy-hot. Scintillating. Cool, warm, wet.

Clarice struggled to raise her hand off the bed. She wouldn't give up this fight until she'd reached her goal. Her clit was right there, nearly touching Angel's neck, but she couldn't get it. Couldn't... quite...

I give up, Clarice thought. She would have said it if her mouth would only move.

But Angel must have read her mind, because a soft, smooth thumb brushed her clit. She gasped, pressing her ass harder against Angel's face, forcing the stranger's tongue deeper down in her hole.

Angel brushed her clit again, then rubbed it with perfect pressure. Just what she was looking for. Clarice seized for a moment, then bucked back at Angel's face. This woman must have been *strong like bull* to keep from falling over with all this frenzy going on.

Clarice might not be able to reach her own cunt, but she could certainly grab hold of Angel's. She took the woman by surprise, striking her slick slit and inserting one finger, then two.

Angel's pussy was incredibly wet, but not very tight. Lord, what did that girl put in there? Clarice could insert three fingers no problem, then four, and then... no... was this really happening?

When Clarice curled her thumb within her other fingers, Angel's cunt opened up like a flower to let her in. She pushed her fist inside the stranger's pussy and just held it there, not knowing what to do.

Angel turned around and flopped on the bed so Clarice was on top, one hand shoved in the stranger's cunt, the other finding its way toward her breast. Angel pulled her tongue from Clarice's asshole and sucked it instead. The pressure and the pull felt so strange in combination with that icy-hot tingle that she nearly lost her mind. Her body started thrusting and flopping. It was no longer enough to plant her fist inside this woman's vagina. She had to fuck it, now, and fuck it hard.

This would be impossible with a human. Only angels could take a fist like this.

Angel moaned wholeheartedly as she sucked Clarice's asshole. It felt so good in that moment she might even have found her orgasm without the stranger's thumb on her clit—but she was certainly glad it was there.

The angel stroked her swiftly and lapped her hole until she filled the room with the sounds of orgasm. Her screams didn't bounce off the wall the way Angel's had, but it had been so long since she'd come she didn't care how she sounded. She writhed on the woman's body, feeling those perky nipples and luscious breasts pounding against her pelvis as she pulled her fist from that metaphysical pussy.

She's never slapped a woman's cunt before, and she didn't know why she was doing it now. It just seemed like the thing to do. So she smacked it hard, making Angel scream and shout. The choral orgasm echoed off the walls while Angel went wild on her ass, spreading so much salve she knew she'd be healed.

Even so, when she rolled off the stranger's naked body, she asked, "How does this work? Your tingly saliva makes my ass all better and you fade away into nothingness?"

Angel looked like a dream as she chuckled, her hair a messy cloud on Clarice's pillow, her big breasts bouncing with every laugh.

"Sorry," Clarice said. "I meant to say you're going back to heaven. That's where angels come from, right? Heaven?"

Grabbing hold of Clarice's clean hand, the stranger said, "I'm your Anal Angel. I'll be here to heal you for as long as you've got that bottle of tincture. I hope you don't mind sharing a bed."

Some distant breeze whistled in Clarice's ears and she tried to puzzle those pieces together. She looked toward the window to make sure that was the real world out there and she wasn't simply dreaming, but the curtains were closed.

She shook her head. "Wait, what are you saying?"

"I'm yours," Angel said, holding Clarice's hand against her cool cheek. "I belong to you. I'm your Anal Angel."

"You're mine... like a pet? Like I have to feed you and clothe you?"

"You clothe your pets?" Angel asked.

"Well, no, I don't have any pets, but that's not the point."

Angel answered the question. "You don't have to feed me. I don't eat." A blush crossed her cheeks. "Well... I don't eat food, let's say. And as for clothing me, that's entirely up to you. If you want to keep me naked, I'll be happy that way too."

Clarice gazed into the stranger's mysterious turquoise eyes. She couldn't suppress her feelings of arousal as she snuck a peek at the woman's impressive body. With a girl like Angel in her bed, she'd never sleep again.

"I don't know how I'm going to explain this to my roommates," Clarice said.

"Oh, they won't be able to see me," Angel assured her.

"But they'll sure be able to hear us going at it."

"Well..." Angel's blush deepened. "That's true."

For a moment, the stress of the situation made Clarice's ass clench, but when it did, she felt the tingly coolness of Angel's healing tongue, and her buttocks relaxed. Maybe the medicine wouldn't work one hundred percent on the first try. Maybe they'd have to replay the ass-eating again and again—every morning, noon, and night if that's what it took.

But, for now, Clarice dove at Angel's big, bouncy breasts and sucked those pretty purple tits while a chorus of angels filled her ears.

You might also enjoy:

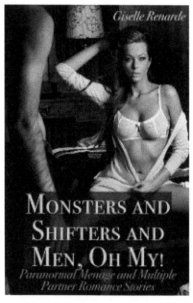

Monsters and Shifters and Men, Oh My!
By Giselle Renarde

JUST CAN'T GET ENOUGH? *Monsters and Shifters and Men, Oh My!* is a box set full of spicy paranormal romances.

Inside you'll find a princess in hiding, a forest full of shapeshifters and a faery with a secret. Curious about that mysterious man at the coffee shop? So are baristas Saada and Toby. Meanwhile, paranormal investigators Geoff and Anna are northward bound to search for the legendary Shadow

People. And how will Artemis react when she encounters a cunning incubus who knows what he wants... and takes it?

Still craving beastly men? Good thing this collection includes a bonus werewolf tale by renowned author Savannah Reardon!

Monsters and Shifters and Men, Oh My! includes two novellas, three novelettes and one short story devoted to menage and multiple partner romances.

Now Available!

ABOUT THE AUTHOR

G iselle Renarde is an award-winning queer Canadian
writer. Nominated Toronto's Best Author in NOW
Magazine's 2015 Readers' Choice Awards, her fiction has
appeared in well over 100 short story anthologies, including
prestigious collections like Best Lesbian Romance, Best
Women's Erotica, and the Lambda Award-winning collection
Take Me There, edited by Tristan Taormino. Giselle's juicy
novels include Anonymous, Cherry, Seven Kisses, and The
Other Side of Ruth.

Giselle Renarde
Canada just got hotter!
Want to stay up to date? Visit
http://donutsdesires.blogspot.com[1]!
Sign up for Giselle's newsletter: http://eepurl.com/R4b11
Weekly Audio Erotica at http://Patreon.com/AudioErotica

---

1. http://donutsdesires.blogspot.com/

2

9 798223 434443